SHANE'S REDEMPTION

Maura's Men Book 3

Stella Williams

SHANE'S REDMPTION

This is a work of fiction. Names, characters, places, and incidents either are the product of the author's imagination or are used fictitiously. Any resemblance to actual persons, living or dead, events, or locales is entirely coincidental.

Editing
Raw Book Editing
www.rawbookediting.com

Book Cover Design
GermanCreative on Fiverr

Publisher
Serpentine Creative LLC
www.serpentinecreative.com

Print ISBN: 978-1-953917-08-9
Ebook ISBN: 978-1-953917-07-2

Author's Note

This story has themes of substance abuse and trauma centered around physical and mental abuse. Readers who are sensitve to these topics please be aware.

PROLOGUE

Molly moved closer to Shane as a cold wind blew. He was tall and slender with the lean muscle mass of a runner despite his life as an academic. Not much of a shield from the cooling weather, but that didn't mean being closer to him didn't warm her in other ways. Winter was almost here. The perfect time for her change since it would give her a plausible reason to not be outside during the transition period.

They were just leaving the steakhouse she'd chosen for her last meal as a human. She'd ordered a salad because she'd watched enough shows to know what happened when someone died. She didn't want a full belly when the moment finally came. That and her nerves were so bad she'd barely been able to stomach the few pieces of lettuce she consumed that evening. Molly almost envied Cat and Claude for the steaks they had ordered.

"We don't have to do this tonight. I'll understand if you need more time," Shane said, running a hand through his shaggy, brown locks.

Molly studied Shane for a moment and wondered

if she would see him differently after the change. For dinner, he'd attempted to brush his hair into a sleek style. His nervous habit had quickly ruined that effect. It now stuck every which way in the windblown, devil may care look that had won her heart the moment she'd met him. Molly hated that he looked so tired and worried. She much preferred when Shane smiled. It made the shadows in his eyes seem softer and less present. Shane didn't smile often. A habit she supposed for hiding his true self.

Shane was a Vampire. When he'd first told her, she believed him instantly. In the short time, she'd known him, Shane hadn't seemed the lying type. He was honest and straightforward with his actions and intentions. Besides, at that point, Molly had already fallen hard for Shane. He could have told her he was an alien from space sent to murder the universe, and she would have gladly been his first victim. She felt that deeply about him.

"I don't need any more time to know that I want to be with you. Are you having second thoughts?" Molly asked.

Shane was a handsome man, and he had a good heart despite what happened to him and the others. Being stolen from their lives and held captive by a vindictive nightmare of a woman. Being forced into exile because of some arbitrary connection to her. Molly was all too aware of what it was like to be unwanted. To be an outcast for things beyond your control. Not to say that being an orphan and being teased because of your red hair and freckles was on the same level as literally living life being marked for death. Shane hadn't gone into detail, but Molly knew this wasn't an easy decision for either of them to make. She didn't want him to regret her, not ever. That thought gave Molly a brief moment of panic.

"You know I want nothing more than to spend my life with you," Shane said.

He put his arms around Molly and guided her towards the car. As always, Shane was the perfect gentlemen. Cat and Claude walked a few feet behind them. Giving them space even though Molly could still feel Cat's glare on her back. Molly knew Cat wasn't happy with this plan. Cat wasn't sold on the whole Vampire thing. It wasn't like her turning would take Molly away from her. Shane had assured Molly that she could continue her friendship with Cat for as long as Cat was willing. He'd avoided saying alive.

Shane knew Molly and Cat were best friends for life. Nothing, not even death, could ever tear the two of them apart. It was one of the reasons Molly had insisted that Shane bring a friend along for this evening. She'd hoped maybe Cat would fall in love too, and they could be Vampire best friends forever. She hadn't expected him to bring Claude of all people.

She knew his friend circle was limited, being one of Maura's Men, but she'd hoped for someone other than Claude. Maybe Xander or even the Felix guy he'd mentioned in passing once. Felix was a professor and historian, which may have bored Cat. Molly had no idea what he looked like since Felix was away in Scotland. Judging by the men Molly had met, Maura was a woman of discerning taste in the looks department.

Xander would have been a hard sell. He hadn't been happy about Molly's relationship with Shane. The massive warrior had none of Shane's modern people skills. Xander would have sat in silence, looking surly right along with Cat. On second thought, maybe Claude had been the better choice. He was an asshole, but at least he had Cat talking and not focusing on Molly being turned that evening. Cat's disapproving attitude was already putting a damper on what should have been a happy occasion.

"I have no idea why any woman would be willing to choose you for eternity," Cat scoffed at Claude, and Molly cringed.

Molly felt Shane stiffen beside her, and she pulled him to her for a kiss.

"Let's hurry to the mansion. Maybe Xander will have better luck in taming Cat, and we can finally be together forever," she sighed.

Shane smiled and kissed her again before opening the car door for her.

"Together forever, my love," he said.

Molly should have felt giddy and excited, but unease gnawed at her insides as soon as Shane shut the door behind her. Tonight was the Vampire equivalent of her wedding night. Something wasn't right about the atmosphere, and it had nothing to do with the winter chill. She hoped it was nothing but bridal jitters.

"Together forever," Molly breathed to herself.

BREAKING POINT

*G*ray. *Everything around her was gray. A fog, like a warm blanket, both comforting and suffocating as it enveloped her from every angle. Something had gone wrong. The last thing Molly remembered was trying to persuade Cat to be part of her Turning and then a bright light. The car must have crashed, but the thought didn't scare Molly as much as it should. If this were the limbo between life and death, then it wouldn't be long before Shane brought her back.*

Molly lay entirely still, smiling nervously in antic-ipation. Waiting for the pull of reality to set in. Shane would bring her back shortly, completing the transi-tion. Molly wasn't looking forward to the pain that would soon come, but if it meant she could be with Shane forever, she was willing to do anything. Shane told her a little about what death and the change would feel like, but this was something different. He'd said it would be painful, quick. This was anything but.

I hope Cat is okay.

Molly didn't see or feel the presence of anyone else, which reassured her that Cat, although in pain, was very much alive. Cat was her best friend and hated the idea of Molly becoming a Vampire. She didn't believe in happily ever after, and given their upbringing, Molly couldn't exactly blame her. Still, Cat had been such a good sport about Shane being a Vampire and everything, even if it was only to make Molly happy. Molly took a deep breath or at least tried to. It felt like cotton balls in her nose as she attempted to suck in air.

What is taking so long?

Doubt began to creep in as the gray became more stifling and the warmth of the light faded. She studied her hand once pale as cream now seemed to be fading, merging with her surroundings. Shane wasn't coming. Her escape from the gray was becoming less and less likely as the light dimmed and a new darker space appeared. Panic began to set in, her heart racing in her chest, shallow, choppy breaths grasping for air, for life. Wispy, curling fingers of darkness converged upon her.

Molly forced herself up and started to move toward the light, but as she tried to get closer, the light grew dimmer and moved further from her reach, all while the darkness gained on her. The gray, like a thick sludge sticking to her frame, made it almost impossible to move any faster, but still, she tried. Chilling tendrils swirled virtually effortless behind her, dogging her heels, teasing her as she clawed and reached for salvation.

The gray seemed to close in on her, sucking her back, pulling her towards the darkness. Molly stretched and strained, reaching for the faint glow in the distance her fingertips could feel its welcoming warmth. She was mere inches from grabbing hold when the gray gave a final tug. The darkness enveloped her, sucking her back like a black hole. Drag-

ging her into the abyss. Her skin began to tingle and then burn, sharp, shooting needles of fire racking across her entire body. She screamed, but there was no sound, only darkness and pain like she had never experienced before.

Molly sat up gasping for air, her whole body stiff and aching as she took in her surroundings. She was no longer in the car with Shane and Cat, nor was she in Shane's room at the mansion. The room was small and thankfully lit only by the dim glow of candles as her eyes burned from even that tiny amount of light.

"Good you're awake." An unfamiliar female voice said from a shadowed corner. Molly froze as the woman leaned closer to a candle, the soft, flickering light highlighting sharp, unfriendly features. The woman smiled, flashing a set of fangs that didn't quite help Molly's peaking unease.

Where am I, and where the hell is Shane?

Molly tried to speak, but her throat felt like it had been scratched raw by a pack of cats. She brought her hands to her throat, searching for physical scars but felt no pucker or scaly scab, only smooth skin.

"It will be a few hours before you are completely healed. That bastard Shane did a real number on you," the woman spat.

Molly didn't miss the venom that dripped from her tone. There was definitely a history between the two, which could only mean one thing. The woman in front of her was the infamous Maura. The woman who had turned Shane and the others. Not that Shane ever talked about it. She had overheard only part of the story when Shane brought Molly to meet Xander and

Claude for the first time. From what little she'd heard, Maura should be the last person greeting Molly at the moment. Something had gone horribly wrong indeed. That or...her stomach heaved, bile rising in her throat only causing it to burn more. Molly didn't dare think of the alternative.

Molly's eyes fluttered open with a groan. Her alarm clock saving her from reliving that painful moment once again. The moment she'd awoken to find that her lover and her friend had abandoned her. Left her vulnerable and at the mercy of Maura of all people. Molly slapped at her alarm, silencing the shrill ringing tone before tossing the covers away from her body. At least that memory was far more pleasant than the dreams the Shadow saw fit to torment her with. Dreams full of flame and damnation that left her sweaty and exhausted. Just the thought of the Shadow made Molly's day worse. Enough was enough already. Shane wasn't the man she once loved, nor was she still the naïve little girl he'd fallen for. Forcing them together now after everything just wasn't going to happen. At least not without some significant changes for both of them. Starting with Molly finally getting everything with her club off the ground. Club Obelisk was her key to freedom, her independence from men, from Maura, and most importantly, from Shane.

Molly checked her phone to make sure no emergencies were awaiting her with the start of the night. At least that's what she told herself. In reality, she was really checking to see if Brody had made contact. Seeing nothing but a calendar reminder about the upcoming meeting with the Council, Molly set her phone back down with a sigh. Like she even needed a reminder about that. Her subconscious may be preoccupied with the past, but her conscious mind was spastic about the Council.

When Molly decided to purchase the bar from the previous human owners, she'd learned a great deal about the business. Not only from a human standpoint but from a Vampire one as well. One couldn't exactly use their human identity and accounts when they were legally dead. Brody had helped her navigate the back channels and under the table negotiations to procure the proper licensing and such.

Molly thought everything was set until she'd received the missive from the Vampire Council. Brody had mentioned them several times, but she hadn't realized just how influential they would be in her quest for independence. Molly was just finishing her morning coffee spiked with a dash of O neg when she received a text from Gretchen.

The replacement bartender bailed. Having Shane cover the bar again tonight.

Molly sighed and text back. Fine.

With Mack out of town and the stress of the Council's impending visit, Molly was forced to take up Shane's open offer to help around the club. She'd definitely taken for granted Mack and his expertise not only as a bartender but as a human in the know. He was a master potion maker and had a way of putting even the most skeptical of Vampires and rowdiest humans at ease. He'd really put her in a lurch with his recent penchant for disappearing. Finding someone who could recreate his cocktail menu and not accidentally serve any real Bloody Mary's to a human patron was quite taxing.

Shane was okay in a pinch but having him around opened up its own can of worms. It was yet another way her past was coming back to bite her in the ass. At first, she'd thought it would dampen the little business that had dared stick around after last week's altercation with Maura. Instead, Shane's presence seemed to bolster it. His grim reaper looks were a hit with the human crowd who'd already brought in a semi-goth theme to the club. It was also a novelty for the other Vampires to be in such close proximity to one of Maura's Men, especially one who was serving them.

Shane, of course, was always there for her, minus the one time it had honestly mattered. Brody, on the other hand, had been suspiciously absent since the altercation with Maura. Not that they had any sort of relationship, but Molly couldn't help the feeling of abandonment that set in when her lover hadn't returned her calls. If she could even call him that. She had a strict no penetration rule that she had been surprised he had agreed to. Not that he hadn't tried to push the bounds once or twice. Molly chugged the rest of her morning meal before heading to the club. It was going to be a long night.

❋❋❋

Club Obelisk was one of the last places Rodney wanted to be, second only to Maura's presence. In both, he had about an equal chance of having his head ripped off. The only difference being at least the traitors would kill him quickly. Maura would take her time destroying his mind first and then his body. She already was killing him slowly with her insane demands and insatiable appetite for blood. Maura's orders were clear. Keep the flow of intelligence and food constant or his ass was on the chopping block.

Rod did his best to blend into the shadows of the crowded club as he made his way to his spot for the night. He was thankful that Molly had played up the Goth aspect of the club, focusing the flashing beams of light on the center of the dance floor and the bar, filling it with dark, shadowy places. Perfect for hiding, among other things. His vantage point was the second-best viewpoint of the club. Along the wall by the entrance. Close enough to see who came and went with a clear view of the bar and the raised VIP platform but far enough into the crowd to not be noticed.

Both humans and Vampires alike crowded the dance floor at the center of the space and pressed against each other at the main bar on the back wall. The usual bartender was nowhere to be seen. Instead, interestingly enough, the gangly traitor was behind the bar, looking like a knock-off Grim Reaper as he tossed back almost as many shots as he doled out to customers. He smirked, seeing Vampire Lite pull a small packet of something out of the tip jar. No telling what was in there, but Rodney knew a drug deal when he saw one.

Molly, the club owner and the reason Rod was risking life and limb in the shadows, was standing at the railing of the VIP section. It was positioned between the main bar and the hall leading to the employee area. Molly's eyes were sharp and focused as she scanned her club. Surveying everything as if she were the queen and the patrons her loyal subjects. It wouldn't be a complete stretch. It unnerved him how similar she was to Maura. Not in looks. Molly's fiery gaze and pale complexion were the complete opposite of the ambiguous ethnicity and soulless depths of Maura.

It was all in the attitude. The way she commanded the attention of those around her. How the sea of people instinctively parted as she walked through. Not a single person daring to touch her. As if her touch could mean death, and that was entirely possible. The humans in the club may be none the wiser, but rumors of Molly's power spread like wildfire amongst the Vampire community.

Rod himself had firsthand knowledge of that power, and frankly, he had no intention of getting a second glimpse of it either. Had it been directed at him instead of Maura, he'd surely already be dead, or whatever it was that Vampires did. He slunk further into the shadows as he noticed the other two traitors enter the bar. While the blond one and the creepy one frequented the place because of their mates, it was the gladiator's presence that intrigued him the most. He pretended to be some stuck-up businessman, but Rod had seen him fight. Seen what happened when his switch was flipped. Thank god this was solely a reconnaissance mission.

Nothing seemed to be happening tonight, and with all three of the traitors in the building, the place reeked of hostility as the Vampires in the area went on red alert. It was time for Rod to leave. He wouldn't go unnoticed if he stayed any longer, especially with the other Vampires being hyper-vigilant. Rod emanated Maura's presence like a red flag to a bull. The traitors weren't the only Vampires he had to worry about.

He ducked out of the club and headed down the street. With his spying gig over, it was time to grab some munchies. Not for him, of course. He had to wait until his mistress was satisfied before he could dare feed himself. He should have snagged a laced drink from the club, but with the Silence of the Lambs behind the bar, he hadn't risked it.

The tension between the traitors had been palpable. Maybe they would do him a favor and knock each other out of the running. Either way, it was something he could report back to Maura. Maybe now was the time to strike. They weren't as unified as she thought, and that discord was just the thing to put an end to this whole mess. Get rid of the traitors, then get rid of Maura. Rodney nearly fell over as a sharp pain sliced through his brain and down to his toes. Nix that second part. The traitors had to go.

❈❈❈

Molly stood at the edge of VIP, looking out over the crowded dance floor. She nodded at Xander and Claude as they entered and watched as they chose posts giving them a full view of the club while also hiding from the masses. Shane was at the bar serving the eager patrons. Gretchen, as the floor manager, was making the rounds. Checking in with the bouncers and the two waitresses that were gliding through the writhing bodies with tubes of neon escapism. It was calming to see everything running smoothly so far—one less thing for Molly to stress over.

"You look ravishing this evening," Brody said, slipping his arms around Molly's waist.

She stilled at the possessive nature of his embrace, especially in front of Shane, who, despite his emaciated form, was apparently gearing up for a fight. Shane's eyes danced with a crazed light that reminded Molly of the one and only time she'd seen a feral Vampire. Molly turned to face Brody, taking a step back and out of his arms. She was pissed that he thought he could just waltz into her club like he hadn't been MIA the last month. It also didn't feel right. Being affectionate with someone else in front of Shane felt like a betrayal. A slap in the face to what they once shared.

"Brody, long time no see," she said with a pleasant and professional smile.

He smirked and took her arm.

13

"Love, don't be clingy. It's not becoming," he said with a short laugh.

Molly's smile faltered a little.

"She's not the one who seems to have a problem," Shane snarled behind her before she could answer.

Brody glared at Shane before shaking his head in disgust.

"What happened to Mack?" Brody asked, paying no further attention to Shane.

Molly could feel Shane's anger peaking like flaming barbed wire on her back. A feeling she was unfortunately familiar with due to her more intense encounters with the Shadow. She needed to deal with Brody away from Shane. The last thing Molly needed was an altercation between the two. The Council would surely have a field day with that, and as much as she couldn't forgive Shane, he didn't deserve to be put to death over her.

"Let's go to my office," Molly said.

She walked away before either of them could say another word. Molly didn't miss Brody's triumphant smile or Shane's killing glare before Brody followed. As soon as her office door closed, Brody was on her. Pressing Molly against her desk, his hands slid up her skirt to touch her. She pushed him away.

"I didn't invite you here for that." She moved to put her desk between them.

He smirked and took a seat.

"Fine, if you want business first. The Council will be here in two days, and as their liaison, I came to make sure you understood the rules before their arrival," he said.

"Since when are you their liaison," Molly asked.

He raised an eyebrow at her.

"Do you think I approached you just for my own jollies?"

Molly felt sick. Of course, she had been the one to initiate their intimate relationship. Now his detachment made sense. It wasn't because he was okay with her non-committal terms. He had been keeping appearances. Feeling her out, quite literally, for The Council.

"So, you were using me," she stated.

He leaned across the desk towards her.

"If you think for one second that I would agree to such paltry intimacy out of duty, you are completely out of touch," he growled before pulling her into a kiss.

It was different from the times he'd kissed her before. There was no seduction, no playfulness. It was all raw need. It scared her. Vampire men were notoriously possessive, and while Molly had given Brody certain liberties with her body, she thought it had been clear that her heart wasn't in the bargain. Molly had no desire to be possessed by anyone. She'd vowed never to make that mistake again.

❄❄❄

"Hey, buddy. Turn it down a notch or two before you scare the precious few customers away," Gretchen hissed in Shane's ear.

He tore his gaze away from the door that led to Molly's office and begrudgingly turned his attention to the pissed off humans anxious for their poison of choice. Not that he could blame them. He downed a shot of the most potent stuff on the shelves before taking a single order.

Shane didn't care that Gretchen was glaring angrily at him. He never said he was a good bartender, but he had been the only option on such short notice. He didn't mention that it was because he'd scared the other applicants away. No, that would be his secret. He'd needed this piss poor position to get closer to Molly.

The past few months had been torture not being able to see her. Rationally, Shane knew she needed space. Some time to come to terms with everything that had transpired in the last few years. However, in his present state, Shane was far from rational. Fueled by a deadly cocktail of drugs, alcohol, and the primal need to possess her and only her, Shane would do anything for a moment in her presence. The sight of her gave him a better high than anything he could shove into his abused, emaciated body.

Even seeing her flirting with other males in the club had been better than not seeing her face at all. At least it had been until The Council's henchman had arrived. Shane nearly crushed the shaker in his grip when he thought of the familiarity the man seemed to have with her. If Molly hadn't dragged the man away, Shane had no idea what he would have done. Even in his weakened state, Shane would have easily shredded the healthier Vampire for touching his woman.

"Shane," Gretchen snapped, forcing him back to the moment.

His emotions were running so high and fast he hadn't noticed the feral snarl rumbling in his throat. Hadn't realized his lips curled back in a gruesome snarl that revealed his long, sharp canines. It drew the attention of the few Vampires in the room as well as the humans crowding the bar for drinks. The humans were stupidly cheering as if it were some sort of show. The Vampires were bracing for a fight. Shane was their worst nightmare. One of Maura's Men had finally snapped.

Shane had never felt so out of control in his life. Molly was his. There was no way he would just stand idly by while she was taken advantage of by another. He leaped over the bar and made it almost to the office before his friends Xander and Claude blocked his path.

Each grabbed an arm as he struggled against them. Like a caged animal, he jerked and snapped at them with his teeth. Scratched at them with his hands. Still, their combined strength held him at bay as they carried him out the club and away from prying eyes.

Once outside, he was pushed against the brick wall before Claude punched him squarely in the jaw. Shane lunged for him only to be driven back by Xander.

"Your recklessness may have cost you Molly, but if you ever put my female in danger like that again," Claude trailed off, the fire in his eyes enough warning.

Shane seethed, itching for a fight. He struggled against Xander's hold.

"Shane, get a hold of yourself," Xander said as calmly as if he were asking him to pass the salt at dinner, but the undertones were deadly.

Shane hadn't been on anyone's good side as of late. He knew his friends wouldn't hesitate to put him to ground if they thought he was beyond control. The problem was he really couldn't help the primal energy coursing through him at that moment. His entire body had a mind of its own. A drive so intense that despite Xander's strength, his grasp on Shane was tenuous at best. All it would take was a moment of distraction, and there would be no stopping him.

As if sensing Shane's mood, Claude grabbed either side of Shane's head and rammed it into the brick wall with enough force to knock him out. Shane slid to the ground, his friend's curses the last he heard before everything faded to black.

INTERVENTION

"That was a bit excessive," Xander said, hefting an unconscious Shane over his shoulder.

Now back at the mansion, the two men could speak freely. They'd driven back in silence, afraid that their voices might wake Shane sooner than they could get him back. The last thing they needed was an irate Vampire in such close confines.

"The jerk is lucky that's all I did to him. If it had been Cat in there instead of Gretchen, you would have done worse," Claude said, entering the foyer.

His voice echoed a bit in the empty space. The house felt eerily quiet and more somber than it should, considering it housed two mated couples and some extended family.

"Cat would never be in that situation because she knows her place," Xander said, but winced when he turned to find Cat standing behind him. With her hands on her hips and an angry purse to her full lips.

"My place is wherever the hell I feel like, and yours is the floor until I say otherwise. Now take Shane to his room before he wakes and does something we will all regret," she snapped.

Xander took note that she was in the doorway and hadn't come from the direction of the stairs, which meant she hadn't been home like he had expected. He wanted to question her whereabouts but wasn't willing to risk her wrath much further. Instead, he tucked his head and did as he was told, for now.

Heading down the hall toward Shane's area of the mansion, he could hear Cat doing a number on Claude's ego and felt instantly better about his odds of getting back into his bed later that evening. His mate had a temper that burned hot and fast. If she were fanning the flames in Claude's direction, she would be more amiable to him once the issue of Shane was taken care of.

✼✼✼

"Once again, your hero complex rears its ugly head! What were you thinking slamming his head like that?" Cat yelled at Claude, who looked pissed and anxious to head right back out the door.

Cat shoved at Claude's chest, knocking him off balance a little. His head snapped around to face her.

"What's got your tail tonight, Cat? Can't a man be protective of his woman without you biting his head off," he griped.

Cat had been on her way to the club herself when Claude and Xander had returned with an unconscious Shane. The Shadow had been on another one of its rants about Shane and Molly when it had suddenly stopped and demanded she go there straight away. If she hadn't seen their car pull up, she might have just missed them and their little chat about what had happened.

"Look, I get it, finding a mate for you guys is like a miracle, especially for your chauvinist ass, but Gretchen can handle her own. If she needs you, she'll let you know," Cat said.

"Are you done?" Claude asked and started to walk off towards the front door.

"No, I wanted to talk to you about Gretchen's brother as well as Shane once Xander is done putting him to bed. I don't really want Gretchen to be there," she said.

Claude whirled on her.

"Why can't Gretchen be there? He's her brother," he said.

Cat sighed.

"Because I don't want to worry her if it turns out to be nothing," Cat replied.

Claude softened a little in his stance. Cat, of course, had counted on it. He and the others didn't really need to know about her suspicions about the Shadow, but it was on her agenda to be more open about things. Lord knew secrets were what had made all of this mess in the first place. If they all just communicated better, so much could have been avoided. Felix would never have been missing for so long with none of them the wiser. Maura's return would have been noticed sooner or may not have even happened.

Maura would have been so much easier to subdue before now, and without Maura, well, Molly may still have died, but there is a chance Shane may have discovered the secret to bringing her back on his own. They could have had their happily ever after. Gretchen wouldn't have had to suffer Declan's violent attack. For all, we knew she may have ended up with Felix instead of Claude, or better yet, still alive and happy. Her brother, Greg, wouldn't have been caught in Maura's crosshairs either. The Shadow would have never infiltrated Cat's life with her crazy demands. The thought of the Shadow brought Cat back to the present.

"Look, I know you all are worried about him not being himself, but he wasn't with Maura that long. Hell, I'd be more worried if he was acting as if nothing was wrong. The guy just learned about Vampires and has had to give up his entire life because of it. You know how shitty that transition can be," Claude said.

"I do, and it's not that at all. Look, let's just focus on the more pressing issue right now. We need to have a serious discussion about Shane, and it cannot wait a moment longer," Cat insisted.

Cat had chickened out again. There was no bringing up the Shadow at this time. What the Shadow told her about the key to destroying Maura once and for all would stay a secret for now. Maybe it was for the best. The Shadow was still harping about Shane and Molly getting back together. She had yet to mention anything about the Greg plot twist in this whole quest to find love for all of Maura's Men. Then again, that edict had also not been extended to the two douche nuggets that had fought alongside Maura in the last battle. Still, she thought it would be easier to discuss it with Claude since he was the most skeptical of all of this.

"Fine, just give me a minute to work off some of this negative energy, and I'll meet you guys in the library," Claude said.

Cat smiled and gave Claude a quick hug before heading off to make sure Xander was taking every care with Shane. For all the butting of heads they did, it wasn't lost on Cat that she would be dead if it hadn't been for Claude. His blood had given her a new life. That made them family. They were all family, dysfunctional and full of drama just like any other. The Shadow and the question of Greg could wait. Shane's needs were definitely a priority.

❋❋❋

Xander hadn't set foot in Shane's area of the mansion for almost a year. The men had divided the mansion into four sections when they first bought it. Claude and Xander shared the upper floor while Shane and Felix split the lower. At least when Felix was alive. Now the lower east wing was a mostly empty guest space. Not that Felix had done much personalizing. He'd hired a decorator who'd made the place look "Martha Stewart Chic," as he'd said.

Xander personally thought it looked like a cheap motel and wasn't worth even half the designer's ridiculous fees. Not that Shane's idea of decorating was any better. The late sixties, early seventies weren't the best of design decades. At least Shane had the decency to keep the motif behind closed doors. The hallway itself matched the original design of the place: clean white walls and marble flooring.

Shane's increasingly erratic behavior should have been enough warning. Yet Xander's occupation with pleasing his mate had left Shane to wither almost unnoticed. His ordinarily clean workspace was piled with trash and paraphernalia. Pill bottles, both empty and some tipped over onto a shard of glass. A few were still whole while others were crushed and forming neat lines. Some glass tubes and burnt spoons reminded Xander of the opium dens he'd hunted in during their time with Maura. Dried mushrooms and the antique water pipe that had disappeared from the study were by Shane's bed.

The sharp aroma of chemicals and body odor on soiled linens was unbearable. The entire scene reminded Xander of one of those awful hoarding shows that Cat and Gretchen were obsessed with. Adjusting Shane's weight Xander took him down the hall to Molly's old room. The only place untouched by his apparent disregard for hygiene. Until his space was habitable again, this would be where he stayed.

In the old days, Shane would never have been allowed to get so low. Shane would have been staked or worse at the first hint of mental illness. The Vampire world wasn't nearly as forgiving as the human one. Especially to those like Shane, Claude, and himself, whose image was already tarnished by the nature of their sire. The decision had to be made. There was no way Shane could continue to go unchecked. From that moment on, Shane would be monitored every minute of every day until they figured out a way to work out his issues.

Once Shane was snuggly tucked into bed, Xander walked back through each of Shane's rooms. He surveyed the damage and opened the windows. The night breeze wasn't strong, but any wind was better than none when it came to ridding the area of that smell. Even years of living amid the stench of death could not have prepared his nose for Shane's rooms. With that done, Xander made his way to the study where he knew Claude and his mate would be waiting. Who Xander didn't expect to see were Mack and Greg. Greg had pretty much holed up in the guest room since he'd woken, and Mack was supposed to be out of town because of the Council's pending visit. How Mack knew so much about the Council and their kind was a mystery that Xander had yet to solve. This, however, was not the time to speculate on that. Shane was a much more pressing issue. Mack so far had proved himself not just trustworthy but useful.

"Mack forgot something at the club and saw you two lumbering away with Shane across your back. He was afraid something bad had happened," Cat explained, coming to his side.

"Something bad has happened. I've failed him. We have all failed him. As pressing as the threat of Maura is, Shane is now our new priority. He should have been our priority for a while now." Xander took a deep breath, feeling the weight of his words like a boulder on his chest.

It was a special kind of torture that he had once again allowed Maura to cloud his judgment towards someone he cared for. It was a festering wound, one that no amount of time had been able to fully heal.

"First order of business. We clear out Shane's space. Cat, I know you have been itching to update something in this mansion. A change of scenery might be just what Shane needs to shock him back to reality," Xander continued.

Cat's eyes lit up for a moment before sighing and shaking her head.

"As much as I would love to rid the theater room of shag carpeting. That isn't going to help Shane. It will only make things worse because we will have lost his trust. We can't be of any help unless he trusts us." Cat began to pace and worry her lip.

Xander could almost see the gears working in her head as she fought to control her emotions and find a solution that would best help Shane. A sense of pride swelled in his chest. His mate had been the glue to hold their very dysfunctional family together for the past few years. She'd cared for Shane and kept him sane as long as she could on her own. She'd managed Claude's ego like a pro and helped him find happiness with Gretchen. She'd done so much for all of them without asking a single thing in return. She hadn't asked for this life. She'd been turned without permission, and yet Xander couldn't help but be thankful.

In a way, Shane's downfall had been his rebirth. If the crash that had stolen Molly from Shane and started this horrific chain of events hadn't happened, Xander would never have had the opportunity to claim the magnificent woman he now called mate.

"Fuck trust. We can worry about that when he isn't some bleary-eyed lunatic. He is far beyond reasoning at this point. We have to take drastic measures now, or we will have to put him down. Bad enough we have to deal with one crazy Vampire. I'm not risking—" Claude didn't get to finish as Cat slapped him.

"Don't you dare suggest that Shane is anything like that bitch! What is wrong with you? Shane is our family! How could you even think about killing him?" she fumed.

Claude turned a solemn gaze on Xander before his attention returned to Cat.

"You didn't see him tonight. Never in all of my years, including my time with Maura, have I seen any Vampire that..." Claude struggled to find the right words.

"Tortured, violent, out of control, a single-minded focus on destruction," Xander finished for him.

"You agree with him!" Cat glared at him.

So much for not provoking her wrath tonight. Xander should have had the others leave. Greg was new to being a Vampire. He had his own things to deal with. Mack was an exceptional resource but also an outsider. Neither one of them had a stake in this. Cat and Claude proceeded to bicker, and Xander just wasn't in the mood to break it up at the moment. Even if he knew it wasn't helping them find a solution.

Greg cleared his throat, but it was clear Cat and Claude were too busy arguing to notice. Greg crossed the room to stand between the two.

"Look, I'm new to all this, but from what Gretchen told me, you Vampires have a whole set up just like humans. So, don't you have some kind of rehab program we could send him to?" he asked.

"Not that I am aware of. The Turned Vampires don't

have much in the way of a family structure. Purebloods would be too wary of admitting any weakness in their bloodline. Anyone showing this extreme lack of control would be locked away until they died or put to immediate death," Xander said.

As he spoke, Xander noticed Mack shaking his head.

"Maybe about fifty years ago, but the human drug problem has spread far enough to the Vampire community that there have been some changes. They don't have their own facility, but they have worked out a deal with a prestigious human one. If you can afford the fees, that is an option," Mack said.

Claude chuckled.

"Of course, Mr. Encyclopedia of all things paranormal would know this," Claude said, "Still, we are tainted by Maura's blood. We aren't accepted in the Vampire world. If anything, they would be more likely to take the chance to kill Shane rather than help him."

"The place is run by humans. They don't care about Vampire politics, only about the money. If you want extra assurances, we can register him with false identification," Mack suggested.

Xander looked around the room for a moment before sighing heavily. He didn't like the idea of Shane being out there so vulnerable, but he also couldn't ignore the fact that without professional help, Shane may have to be put to death. Xander couldn't imagine the damage that would do to the small family they had formed over the years. Shane was like a brother to him, closer even. There was no real choice to the matter.

"How soon can he—" Xander began before Cat cut him off.

"The risk is too great. I can't let you ship Shane off when we are all perfectly capable of handling things here. It's our fault that we let him get this bad, and it's our responsibility to help him get better. If the humans at that facility can be bought so easily, how can we trust them? Besides, it wouldn't take much for another Vampire in their care to recognize Shane as sired by Maura."

"That is true. Even the newest of Vampires have a way of sensing her evil within us," Claude sighed.

Cat squeezed Xander's hand. He wasn't sure if it was to reassure him of this decision or to reassure her that they could handle it together.

"You guys do have an aura about you. I wouldn't call it evil per se but more an extreme magnetism. More so than any other Vampire I've come across," Mack agreed.

"Not saying I'm a miracle worker or anything, but I did my fair share of relationship and addiction counseling while I was serving. I could be of some help to Shane if I can get him to open up to me," Greg chimed in.

"Alright, Shane is staying, but first we need to clean his room," Xander said, hating that he sounded more like a frustrated parent than a concerned friend.

"Look, I'm the first to admit that Shane is off his rocker, but I don't think we should be the ones making this decision. I think we should see what Shane thinks," Claude said, surprising everyone, especially Xander.

Claude wasn't usually the type to sit around for other people to make a decision. He had a very take-charge personality, but then again, Xander knew that finding a mate had a way of changing you without you even knowing. If the women weren't so involved in Shane's well-being, Xander would have put him to ground without hesitation. After the atrocities they'd all been through, the men had discussed the possibilities of one or all of them losing their senses. One could never be too careful given their demonic sire.

"If he were capable of making that decision, he would have done it himself long before now," Xander argued.

"All I'm saying is we should ask him first. It won't matter if we force him into getting help and he's not ready," Claude said.

"I agree with that one. You can lead a horse to water, but you can't make it drink," Greg chimed in.

"I need to leave soon. I can take Shane with me to the facility tonight, but that's it. I really must be going," Mack said, checking his watch for the fifth time since the discussion had begun.

"Well then, I guess we better wake him up," Cat said and marched out of the room before Xander could stop her.

He cursed under his breath before following her out. He loved Cat more than anything, but sometimes he wished she were of a more demure nature. It would make moments like these so much easier. Still, he made no move to stop her, just tagged along in case Shane needed to be restrained once again.

REVELATION

Molly should be at the club, not sitting like a psycho outside of the Mansion where her best friends lived with their mates. The same mansion where Shane lived. Where she would have lived if things had gone to plan. Molly rested her head on the steering wheel. Now wasn't the time to go through that scenario again. It was in the past, and this was about the future. Not even the future, really, but just the present. Something terrible was happening, and Molly couldn't afford to be out of the loop.

"Just go inside already. Just go and make sure everything is fine, and then you can leave."

Molly attempted a pep talk. When she'd seen Claude carrying a limp Shane out of the alley on the security camera feed, her heart had nearly stopped. Molly immediately kicked Brody out of her office and ran every light on the way to the mansion. She had to make sure Shane was okay. That he was still alive. Molly could tell herself all she wanted that she didn't care about Shane, but she absolutely did. Her heart still very much belonged to him. If anything happened to him... Molly felt the tingling of power rising up and hovering just below the surface. As if her feelings were a physical threat that she needed to be protected from.

She took a few long steady breaths. Doing her best to calm her nerves. To ease the tension and hopefully diffuse the magic threatening to overwhelm her. It was more work than she anticipated. Sweat glistened on her brow, and she quickly wiped it away. After a few more minutes, she decided it was a lost cause. Her emotions were too out of control, and she couldn't guarantee the safety of her friends when she was like this. She reached for the keys to start her car when her phone buzzed. She dug in her purse for her phone and saw the text from Gretchen.

Have you made it yet? Is Shane okay?

Molly sighed. Gretchen could have easily messaged her mate for the information. If Claude wasn't cluing Gretchen in, that meant things really were bad. Claude did everything he could to keep Gretchen safe, both physically and emotionally. Molly hadn't even told Gretchen where she had been going, but Gretchen was always the observant one. A skill Gretchen learned while working with Felix in Scotland and mastered after her transition. A necessary proficiency to protect herself from making the same mistakes that had gotten Gretchen into this mess along with the rest of them. Gretchen knew more than anyone the struggle Molly felt when it came to her feelings for Shane.

Going inside now. I will let you know.

Molly dropped her phone back into her purse and opened the door of the car like ripping off a Band-Aid. Making this about gathering information for Gretchen instead of facing her feelings for Shane had done the trick. Molly was calm enough to go inside, but her hands still shook slightly as she opened the door to the mansion. The fact that the door was unlocked gave Molly a moment of panic.

Had Maura attacked? Had Maura gotten to Shane? Was he under her spell again? That would explain why Xander and Claude had knocked him out.

Molly stepped into the familiar entryway and headed down the dark hall to the study. The lights were on. A fresh glass of blood was on the side table next to the leather settee. There was no one to be found. Molly started to call out. It was unusual that no one would have come as soon as she came in. That she would have gotten this far into the mansion without Cat coming to greet her or Claude coming to bug her about how late Gretchen worked at the club.

What if Maura was here? It was quiet, too quiet, and the place felt like a funeral home. The air heavy with despair. Was Molly too late? Had they been forced to put Shane down? That thought was like a knife to the heart. Molly focused her senses, and finally, she heard the muffled voices of her friends coming from the direction of her old room. With a sigh of relief, she headed down the familiar hallway—her mind racing with a million different possibilities and none of them good.

***

Shane's eyes drifted open slowly. His head was killing him, but that wasn't unusual. He was used to the effects of abusing his body by now.

"Thank god!" Cat's relieved voice penetrated his psyche.

"Cat? Why are you in my room? Did something happen?"

Shane sat up slowly, letting his brain catch up. He wasn't in his room. Instead, he was in the guest room, Molly's room. He inhaled, hoping to catch a hint of her perfume. Of course, there shouldn't be. It had been months since she'd slept here, and Cat and Gretchen made sure the mansion was in pristine shape. Shane registered the fact that there were others in the small room, but his eyesight was still a bit blurry. The soft light of the lamp was nearly blinding, so he kept his gaze lowered. Shane was apparently off his latest high. He should have taken more than just two of the pills his dealer had slipped into the tip jar for him. Human drugs had a way of dulling his Vampire senses until Shane felt almost human again. Still sad and angry with himself, but at least while high, he didn't have to worry about doing anyone any real harm.

"Look, Shane. You lost your shit in front of humans. You need help," Claude said.

Shane sighed. He only remembered being at the club and then waking up here, nothing else. Maybe this new pill had different side effects. If what Claude said was true. He was lucky he was waking and not staked and buried.

"I'm sorry. I don't remember. Thank you for not staking me," Shane said, although he wasn't entirely sure he wouldn't be better off dead.

Molly didn't want him. He was proving useless in the search for Maura's new hideout. In his current state, Shane wouldn't stand a chance in any fight either. He was a lost cause, and judging by the tension in the air, he knew his friends felt the same.

"Don't thank us yet. We understand that the last few years have been rough for you. We are just as much responsible for your state as you are. So, we have decided to give you a chance to redeem yourself," Xander said.

Shane looked up then and saw the seriousness in each of their eyes. While he'd known Cat, Xander, and Claude were in the room, he was shocked to see Mack and Greg there as well. If they were here, then this was indeed a serious matter. Shane had done his best to keep his troubles to himself as of late. He had obviously failed in that task.

"I'm afraid I'm too far gone for redemption," Shane said.

"No! Don't say that," Molly's voice came from the doorway.

Shane's gaze shot up, and he made contact with hers. He hated seeing the concern there. The tears glistening in the corners of her eyes because of him. Always because of him. He was still letting her down. Maybe it was time for him to let her go. If it were his choice to let her go, then perhaps, he'd get over it faster. Find a better way to cope than poisoning himself. Sure, human drugs didn't do much damage with occasional use, but with the amount and frequency of his current habit, Shane couldn't be sure that no permanent damage had been done.

✤✤✤

As Molly approached the room, the voices she'd heard stopped. They had sounded serious but not panicked, meaning everything was probably fine. Molly had almost turned around to leave. Then she heard his voice, weak and defeated as he declared himself unredeemable. She couldn't go at that point. Her heart wouldn't let her. She stood in the doorway, studying Shane's sad state. When his eyes met hers, she almost didn't recognize what she saw.

No matter how bad he'd been before, he always looked at her with love and longing. Now his eyes were full of sadness, regret, and defeat. He was a broken shell of the man she once loved, which was not okay with Molly. She walked into the room and knelt before

33

him. She reached for his hand, but he pulled away.

"Go, please. I don't want your pity," Shane said.

Molly grabbed his hand anyway. It was cold and frail, and she could detect a slight tremor as he fought with his emotions.

"Good because you don't have it. For the last year, you've been chasing me. Invading my space. Inserting yourself into my daily life. Trying to win back my affections, and I've been a total bitch. I've avoided you and dismissed your feelings. I've been so adamant about you betraying me that I couldn't see how much the last few years has affected you as well," Molly said.

There was a flicker of hope in his eyes, and his loose grip tightened around her hand.

"So, you have noticed," he said.

"I have, and frankly, I haven't liked what I've been seeing. Your drug use and the drinking, I want to be able to forgive you. I just can't when you haven't forgiven yourself. When you insist on destroying everything about you that I once loved. You need help, Shane. I need for you to get help," she pleaded.

"Which is what we are offering," Cat chimed in.

"I can help you here. I have some informal counseling experience from my time in the military. I know we don't know each other well, but if you accept my help, it will require you to trust me with things," Greg said.

"Or you can pack a bag and leave with me tonight. There is a human facility that treats Vampires for a substantial fee. They have a pretty high success rate in treatment, but it's all up to you. You have to want to get better," Mack said.

Shane looked between the two men and then back to Molly.

"Which would you prefer?" Shane asked.

"It's not about me right now, Shane. This is about

you. What do you think you need?" Molly said.

"You. I need you," Shane said and kissed her.

Molly kissed him back. She knew she shouldn't. Molly knew she should probably keep her distance, but she couldn't help it. Her heart missed him, missed this, and part of her knew that this kiss was more than just an expression of lust. He needed this for reassurance. He needed to hope that they could go back to how they were before.

They couldn't, of course. Too much had happened at this point. Molly was a different person, and hopefully, after getting help, Shane would also be. The truth was that they could never be the same, but maybe they could find a way to be different people together once this was all behind them. Molly pulled away with a sigh.

"I need you too. Just not this you. Please, Shane, get help," she pleaded with him.

"Okay, for you, I will," he responded.

"No, Shane, not for me. For yourself. I love you; I will always love you; I just can't promise it will be in the way you want me to. Don't hinge your recovery on getting me back. That's unfair to both of us," Molly said, and she saw some of the hope leave his eyes.

Shane moved his hand from hers, and she felt a piece of her heart fade away like the warmth of his touch.

"Molly, why don't we go talk and let Shane discuss his options further with the guys," Cat said.

Molly didn't really want to go. She wanted to be there when Shane made his decision, but one glance at Cat and she quickly stood and followed her from the room.

"Did you have to say that? You couldn't have just let him hope," Cat tore into her as soon as they were a safe distance from the men.

"Do you want him to get help or not? I gave him hope so that he would go, but I couldn't let him think I'd just jump back into his arms just because. If he relapses, I don't want that kind of Karma on me. He needs to do this for himself," Molly replied, erecting her walls once again.

"So, you have not a single thought of getting back with Shane," Cat asked, fire dancing in her eyes.

Molly had to tread carefully. Cat was in full Momma Bear mode, and Molly didn't want to risk suffering the consequences of poking the bear. Cat had destroyed many a foe on Molly's behalf, and after witnessing the carnage, Molly had no intention of being a victim.

"I don't know. Maybe one day. It's complicated," Molly said.

It was probably best to leave things open-ended. Sure, part of Molly would love to get back to that can't eat, can't sleep, starry-eyed bliss she'd once had with Shane. Together forever had been a wistful sigh from her lips to her heart, but now she wasn't so naïve. She knew better to count on prince charming to swoop in and rescue her. He hadn't rescued her. Molly had saved herself while he'd left her to rot, beheaded in a grave. He'd resigned himself to disintegrate both mentally and physically as he'd abused drugs in a misguided attempt at punishment and grief.

"It really isn't. Either you still love Shane or you don't. You need to figure that shit out, Molly, because you will forever be a danger to him if you're still on the fence," Cat said.

That pissed Molly off. Cat was seriously protecting Shane right now. Choosing to acknowledge Shane's feelings over hers.

"A danger to him! What about the danger he put me in? He tricked me into thinking he would turn me and then left me to die. He left me vulnerable to Maura. He brought this all not just on me but on all of us," Molly ranted.

Cat put a hand on her hip and eyed Molly like she had just lost her mind.

"Are you even listening to yourself right now? Did you forget that fucking beheading is damn near impossible to come back from? Did you forget your own choice to believe Maura's lies? Your willingness to turn your back on Shane and me in your thirst for revenge? I've forgiven you for that. Shane has done nothing but grieve and obsess over winning you back. Honestly, Molly, it's you that needs the fucking help. You're stuck in the fucking past and making piss poor fucking choices because of it."

Cat's words hit Molly like a semi going over one hundred. She was floored not just by the truth in her friend's chastisement but the fact that for the first time since returning home, Molly truly saw things from her friend's point of view. From Shane's point of view. Her eyes began to sting, tears forming once again. Pooling along her lash line before spilling from the corners, a stream of regret.

Molly turned and fled the room. She didn't want to let Cat see that she was right. Molly would never hear the end of it, and frankly, Molly would rather find out what Shane's decision was about getting help. If he chose not to then all of this was for nothing anyway. She could never be with him the way he was now. She headed for Shane's quarters only to stop when she saw him holding a duffel bag and chatting somberly with Xander and Claude by the front door.

"You're leaving?" she asked, walking up to the group.

Shane looked up and smiled softly.

"I've witnessed the effects of detoxing before. I don't think I could handle you all seeing me so broken. Besides, it will be a surprise for you how far I'll have come when I return. It will seem much more impressive if you don't see it in progress," Shane said.

Molly threw her arms around him in a big hug. Shane's arms encircled her and held her close to his sharp bony frame. Molly looked into his eyes and kissed him to keep him from seeing the newly forming tears in her eyes. There was a desperation to the kiss, as both of them knew that this wasn't the right way for them to come together. Yet they held each other tightly, making out until Mack cleared his throat.

"Sorry to interrupt, but we need to get going," Mack said.

Reluctantly, Molly pulled away.

"Will you be here waiting when I get back," Shane asked.

"I can't promise you that. Not just because of everything but because I'm meeting with the Council in two days, and there's no telling how that will go," Molly said.

"Well, that explains the Council's summons," Xander said.

Molly opened her mouth to ask him what he meant by that but was cut off by Cat.

"You guys can discuss that later. Right now, we need to get Shane and Mack on their way," Cat said.

Molly gave Shane one last hug before moving so Cat could do the same. Then he was off.

PREPARATION HELL

Shane was gone. Molly had prayed for a reprieve from his constant presence, but now that he was gone, she felt oddly empty. Even when she'd been under Maura's influence, Molly never thought him absent from her heart. Shane had always been there. Even at times when Molly was seething with hatred towards him.

When she'd returned home to find the broken shell of a man that he had become, the anger had turned to pity and disgust. If he was going to go on without her, he could at least have the decency to do it well. He was supposed to be happy and healthy. Not a miserable intoxicated skeleton. He was supposed to be someone she could fall back in love with. He hadn't been, so she pushed him further away. Clung to her anger instead of falling into despair at the loss of the only man she had ever loved.

How dare he destroy her dream of happiness a second time? How dare her heart still care for the man who'd left her for dead? Who'd conned her into believing the fairy tale of "together forever"?

She was falling down the rabbit hole again. Choosing to deny the truth. Not just about what had transpired after the accident but about her feelings. Molly didn't want to have feelings. She wanted to move on and live an uncomplicated life as a successful club owner and upstanding member of Vampire society. Maura's tainted blood be damned.

Molly sighed and checked the clock that hung on the wall above her office door. Xander should be there any moment. She made her way out to the bar. It was empty as the sun had yet to set, and Mack was out of town until after the Council visit. Molly was exhausted. It was well before her typical waking hours. Still, she hadn't been able to sleep last night. Thoughts of Shane being whisked away to rehab as well as the Shadow's ire.

The Shadow had paid Molly another lovely visit last night. Downright pissed that Shane was so far from her ability to meddle, the Shadow took it out on Molly per usual. Molly rubbed the still tender skin of her arms. Her heightened senses picking up hints of the sickeningly sweet smell of burning flesh. The scent one that Molly was far too acquainted with thanks to that monster. Molly still couldn't believe Cat listened to that thing as if it was the good guy in all of this. For all they knew, the Shadow was the real monster, and Maura was just a poor soul also under its twisted influence.

Molly shook her head with a laugh. Maura was far from innocent and definitely not a woman to be manipulated. Maura was the manipulator, and the Shadow was no better but definitely not worse. At least the Shadow operated under the guise of helping. Maura was a selfish bitch determined to rule the world and destroy anything and everything in her path. The Shadow was probably just a vindictive spirit out for revenge against Maura. That wasn't too much of a stretch. Molly just wished the Shadow was as gentle as it claimed to be benevolent.

Maybe she should bring up the Shadow with Xander when he arrived. Cat could be in grave danger, and if anyone could protect her, it would be him. Granted, Xander didn't like Molly all that much either. They'd reached a truce at this point, but they weren't buddies by any means. He'd be more likely to think her crazy and get rid of her himself than to listen to her ideas about this Shadow character.

"Are you ready?" Xander asked, startling Molly from her thoughts.

Molly turned around with a sigh. She did her best not to wring her hands or bite her lip, both actions a dead giveaway to her nerves. The Council visit was just over a day away. Molly had never been more on edge in her entire life. Even being turned into a Vampire and waking up in Maura's lair hadn't been so terrifying.

"As I'll ever be," Molly sighed.

Xander smirked, flashing a row of pearly whites that would make any other woman swoon, even with his massive canines. Xander was an attractive man, and Molly could totally see why her best friend had fallen for him so quickly. Even without the Vampire charm, he was a sight for the eyes.

"It's okay to be nervous. Don't tell anyone, but I was afraid I might piss my pants when I first faced them," Xander said.

"I find that hard to believe. You survived Maura's horrors. I know I don't know what all that entailed, but I've been in her presence long enough to know it couldn't have been a picnic," Molly replied.

"We aren't here to talk about that. We are here to get you prepared to present your case in front of the Council," he said.

"I know, so where do we begin?" she asked.

"Have you decided to share your abilities with them?" Xander asked.

"They already know. It's one of the reasons I'm so nervous. I don't know how to control it," Molly said.

Xander nodded.

"Then we will start with that," he said.

"I told you I can't control it. I don't know how to make it come out or how to make it go away. It's too dangerous," Molly hung her head.

Usually, she wouldn't feel comfortable showing so much weakness, but he was her best friend's husband. He was one of the few people she knew she could let her guard down around. Had needed to, in fact, multiple times as she'd found her way in the world post-incident.

"Alright, then we can work with that. We won't bring it up. So, the Council as a whole does a pretty good job of governing the Vampire population in this region as I'm sure you've already discovered," he said, taking a seat at the bar.

They'd agreed to meet at her bar because it was the one place they could gather without prying ears and eyes. The mansion, while secure, wasn't the place for this. Cat would be interrupting and weaseling her way into the conversation. Gretchen was far too curious about the Vampire world to be kept away either, and that meant Claude would be right by her side. That was already too much of an audience for Molly's liking. Then there was the issue of Shane. He may not be there at the moment, but there were too many reminders of him at the mansion for Molly to ever be comfortable.

"Yes, a royal bloodline that rules indirectly through appointed councils. Each has a Council that does all the grunt work, so to speak. It's the regional Council with which I will be meeting. They will take their opinions to the ruling family, who will make the final decision. Judging if I can live the life I'm currently enjoying, or if I am to be exiled as you and the others have been,"

Molly recited what she had learned from Brody.

He may have been an asshole, but he'd had his uses. Molly glanced at her office door, remembering their last encounter. When she discovered Brody had been lying to her the entire time. When he'd made it clear he wanted more from Molly than she was prepared to offer. All the other little things that bothered Molly spilled forth. That had spurred on the colossal argument before he'd stormed out of her office and out of her life. Hopefully for good, once this Council business was over and done with.

It probably hadn't been a good idea to have a messy break up with the Council's liaison. Especially before the meeting, but there was nothing she could do about it now. Molly turned her attention back to Xander. He'd been rambling on about the Council members and their personalities despite her obvious distraction. It was relevant information to pay attention to. Knowing your opponent was half the battle.

"I'm sorry, but can you go over that again?" Molly asked.

Xander scowled but started over from the top. With a renewed focus, Molly listened and began to take notes.

"There are five Council members. Northernmost America represented by Kirima. She, and trust me despite her brutish appearance, will probably be the most in your favor. Kirima is what you could call a feminist, but in the extreme," Xander paused as Molly rolled her eyes.

"You would associate a brutish woman with feminism," Molly muttered.

"It is not her appearance, but her beliefs. She believes women should rule the world, and if Maura hadn't been a glutton for beautiful, young women, I'm sure she'd welcome her into polite society with open arms," Xander continued despite her interruption, "The United States represented by Nathaniel will be the most against you. He believes all women should stay in their place. The only boon is that he may spend more time arguing with Kirima than giving you any thought as long as he isn't aware of your power. He may, however, insist that you fall under my jurisdiction because of your connection to Maura."

Molly reached behind the bar and poured them both a cup of blood.

"Great! A feminist and a chauvinist. No need to worry. This will be just like handling you and the others."

"This is serious, Molly! You know that there is more than the fate of your bar at stake here," Xander downed the blood she had poured.

Up until that moment, he'd been playing it cool, but as Molly studied him now. A slight sheen of sweat across his brow. A brow that was creased with worry. He actually cared, and that hit Molly harder than anything else he'd said in the last few minutes.

"I am taking this seriously," she said softly. "I just... I need to find something to poke fun at, or I'm going to lose my shit."

Xander sighed and shook his head.

"You and Shane are a fucking pair, you are," he said.

Molly frowned.

"Let's not bring that up. The Council?"

Molly sat up straight and did her best to look perfectly serious. Xander sighed before moving on with his explanation.

"The Central and Southern representatives Cadmael and Eadrich are twins. They usually share the same opinion, as well as their looks, but don't be fooled. They may be the hardest to turn in your favor. Not because of any personal motives, but your active association with Maura is something they may not be willing to overlook.”

“And the fifth?”

“Maximus. He is mostly there as a tiebreaker. Maximus is a member of the ruling family and represents the purebloods. Don’t focus too much on him. He would prefer we all be killed immediately. It’s rumored that it was his great, great grandfather who sired Maura,” Xander said.

Molly stopped taking notes.

“Killed? Really? If he is a part of the ruling family, how can I expect his opinion not to out rule the others?”

“It didn’t matter in our case. There is no reason to expect any different. Although, at the time, we all were under the impression that Maura was dead. Her reappearance may sway things,” Xander admitted.

One of Molly’s human vendors walked in from the back with a shipment of alcohol. The clinking of bottles as he dropped his delivery at the bar, signaling that time was up.

“We’ll meet one more time before the visit,” Xander said before leaving.

Molly didn’t feel the slightest bit more prepared for the Council visit, but business came first. Council or no Council, without Club Obelisk, Molly was just another one of Maura’s unfortunate victims. She was nobody, an outcast, a threat.

✱✱✱

Rodney did his best to hide his disgust at the carnage before him. This had definitely not been in the brochure. Not that there was one for becoming a Vampire slave. As always, Axel had bitten off more than he could chew. What had seemed the deal of a lifetime was now Rodney’s worst nightmare. Actually,

45

worse than Rodney's worst nightmare. Nothing could have prepared him for the horror that was Maura.

Carefully, he chose his path through the pile of bodies strewn on the floor. Not that it mattered, the penthouse was bathed in the blood of fallen men. A crimson shrine to Maura, their bodies tossed haphazardly across every available space. Some even stacked on top of one another, but for the time being, that is where they would lay. As gruesome as it was, Rodney's task was much worse. He shifted the slender figure of a woman over his shoulder, careful not to wake her. It was the only kindness he could offer before her demise at the hands of Maura.

"You're late," Maura stated, licking fresh blood from her hands.

Axel and the man who owned the penthouse both lay sprawled at her feet. Not dead but close to it after what no doubt was a punishing sexual encounter with their mistress. It didn't matter that she stood before the floor to ceiling windows as this was the only high rise building in the area, and the glass was mirrored on the outside.

Rodney didn't bother to answer. Giving an excuse would elicit a punishment worse than his silence. Maura was brutal with her disciplines. It was one of the reasons Rodney did his best to stay on her good side. Not that it really meant anything. Maura didn't have a good side. It was all bad basking in her shadow, especially in her current mood. She was still pissed and pondering her revenge on the traitors. If it hadn't been for Molly and the blinding light she'd used against Maura. Well, there was no telling what would have become of the world. That bastard Declan had surely gotten the better deal. Being beaten to death by the little, brown-haired mouse of a woman was better than living with Maura any day.

Rodney pushed the thought of that night out of his head. No use dwelling on the past. Maura did enough of that for everyone involved. He carefully set the girl down in front of Maura. Giving her a pinch to the ribs to awaken her. The girl gasped and nearly fainted again at the sight of Maura covered in blood. The girl's obvious horror brought a smile to Maura's face. Even covered in gore, Maura stood regally before them. Like a Queen posing for the admiration of her followers. Any other man would be entranced by her beauty, but Rodney was immune. He knew the cost of that perfectly symmetrical visage, and well, it was more than just the pound of flesh before her.

***

Maura stared out at the street below, formulating her latest plan. The blood of her snack working its magic, smoothing creases that had sprouted near her eyes and mouth as she'd entertained herself with her most recent acquisition. In the past month, she'd gathered an army and gorged herself on young flesh in preparation. After her surprising defeat at that dreadful cabin, Maura had almost descended into madness. She had thought her magic lost, but no, it had been transferred into that unfortunate woman Molly. Rodney had stalked the woman for weeks learning her habits and weaknesses, ready to bring her in for the power transference before an ultimately, delicious death.

Maura couldn't wait to drain her of not just her power but her life. However, the night she had chosen to strike, Rodney had been forced to slink back to her lair. The Council's liaison had come to pay Molly a visit. This development was not good. If the Council got hold of her power, then Maura would be doomed. In her weakened state, Maura was in no position to exact her revenge on the Council. It would do more harm to her plans to even think about attacking at that moment. No, she had to wait and choose the correct time.

The Council would be coming, and it was all a matter of timing. Maura needed her army to be fierce and numerous if she planned to be successful. She wasn't going to rush things like the last time. Her impatience had nearly cost her everything. Molly may have escaped her that night, but it was only a matter of time before Maura had her powers restored. Then, and only then, would she have her revenge on those who had made her in the first place.

Those retched pureblood monsters, who clung to their misguided notions of civility while destroying everything they touched. Maura was their Frankenstein. They had created her, and they would soon pay the price for their arrogance. Maura let herself think back to that fateful night. She'd done exactly what the witch had taught her, except one thing. Maura hadn't been able to stop herself from taking the last drop of blood from her sire. He'd tasted like pure evil on her tongue, but she'd welcomed it—the surge of power, the headiness of revenge, and the stillness of his body. The intense bouquet of fear as his pulse weakened. The final beat of his heart before it crumbled to dust and fell from between her fingers like the sands of time running through the hourglass. It was at that moment that Maura felt genuinely reborn. That her youth and vitality had been restored.

She'd spent years draining humans in a quest for that same high but to no use. The thought of draining the purebloods of their precious elixir of life left Maura panting and salivating in need. A deep hunger grew within her belly, and she knew there was only one thing that could ease the growing ache. Would it quench her never-ending thirst? No, but at least she could have a little fun before the main course.

She swung her foot out, connecting with the mass of male flesh at her feet with a satisfying thud. Her plaything stirred, not daring to look her in the eye. His skin is still marred by their last encounter. If she demanded much more of him, he would surely perish, but she knew he wouldn't shirk away from her. He knew well enough now that his life depended on her continued pleasure with him.

Axel was nothing like his weasel-nosed brother. He knew his place in the grand scheme of things. His loyalty was firmly in her camp. Rodney would learn that soon enough. Maura would relish the look of pure betrayal in his eyes when Rodney's own flesh and blood turned against him in her name.

COUNCIL VISIT

Molly paced outside of the chamber room. It wasn't really a chamber room but the conference room at a large company that was a front for the local Council administration. She'd been here once before to register herself with the Council. Something she hadn't thought necessary, but the Vampires who helped her get home from Scotland had insisted. Until that point, she hadn't realized how big a deal her connection to Maura was. They'd all run from her as if she'd suddenly sprouted a second head. With no one else to turn to, she had gone to the mansion and found Cat. Still, it had been her first significant step toward independence.

Here she was again, although several floors up, making another step towards her goal. Molly was nervous, and it didn't help that Brody was standing next to the guard shooting daggers in her direction. They had taken her phone away as soon as she and Xander entered the building, so she couldn't even pretend to check emails or anything to keep her busy. Xander was inside now, and it was nerve-racking thinking that her time would be next.

Would Xander be allowed to stay with her? Would she face them alone or walk in to be sentenced without even a chance to argue her case? Not that Molly had much of a case. All she had was her heartfelt promise she wasn't anything like the monster who'd brought her back from the dead, and even that was subjective. How could Molly be sure that whatever was inside her hadn't changed her in more fundamental ways? Already she was so much different than the woman she had been before the incident.

Molly was proud of the things she'd been able to accomplish since her resurrection. Coming into her own as a businesswoman. Her club was by far the best venue in town, and she'd basically cornered the market on afterlife clientele. As she was learning more about this new world she'd been brought into, Molly found that there were fewer normal humans that frequented her establishment than she had thought. Of course, Vampires had been less frequent recently due to the Council's scrutiny, but she'd had shifters and even a few magic wielders come to her in thanks for providing a place for them to blow off steam and not feel out of place.

As an orphan, she knew that feeling of being out of place all too well. I guess it shouldn't surprise her that she would find a family of sorts amongst the ultimate of outsiders. She loved what she was doing. As long as the Council was willing to let her live her life, Molly would continue to offer her newfound talent in the entertainment sector to those who needed it most. One of the biggest lessons she'd learned in her experience was that even those who seemed like they had everything going for them needed a place to forget whatever troubled them. Her club had become one of those places for a lot of people, including her.

A shiver went down Molly's spine as a familiar presence registered. She turned around, expecting to see the shadowy figure that had tormented her since her return, only to find nothing. Still, she felt it there as if it were breathing down her neck. Molly had no idea what it was doing there. This had nothing to do with her and Shane, which was pretty much the only thing the Shadow seemed interested in. Molly decided it best to ignore the presence. It evidently wasn't here to set her on fire or rake nails across her skin like before. Honestly, the Shadow was the least of her worries at this point. She would take its torture over the fear of actual death anytime.

"You okay?" Brody asked, startling Molly from her internal pity party.

She looked up to find he'd pushed himself from the wall and was staring at her with genuine concern.

"Yes, thank you," she said with a clipped tone and straightened her posture.

He sighed and shook his head.

"You don't have to pretend to be brave with me. I know you remember," Brody said.

"You don't know a thing about me," she snapped.

"I know that you need to relax. Despite what transpired between us, I gave you a glowing recommendation. I hate to brag, but my word carries quite a bit of weight with the Council. I am their liaison for a reason," he replied calmly as if her anger meant nothing.

Molly bit her lip and let her shoulders relax.

"Thank you, I guess," she said.

Brody snorted and leaned back against the wall.

"If you were really thankful, you'd give me what I want."

Before Molly could reply, the door to the conference room swung open. Xander stepped out, looking surly as ever.

"You're next," Xander said, gesturing for Molly to come inside.

She took a deep breath and strode inside with her

head held high. Xander had told her it was best not to show any sign of weakness or shame. If she wanted to be taken seriously, she would have to prove that she wasn't intimidated by them. That she, and she alone, was in control of herself and thus her future. This was it—the moment she'd been dreading all day.

✻✻✻

Molly stood before the council, trying her best not to laugh at the motley crew before her. Especially when four of the five were sitting in standard office chairs, and the fifth was on a gilded throne. When Xander had described the Council, she'd envisioned a more formidable group. These people in front of her all looked like bad stereotypes. Fur coats, bird feathers, and a spiked leather jacket graced the four Council members. Gilded throne wore an all-black suit, tailored to perfection, but the thick white makeup caked to his pinched face, and powdered wig made it comical. Still, with their gazes trained on her and only her, Molly felt like an animal caged in a zoo.

"This is what all the fuss is about," A large, brutish woman that had to be Kirima said.

"Don't underestimate her, Kirima. That mistake has already been made with her sire," another of the Council members said.

His beady black eyes were skimming over Molly as if she were a pile of excrement at his feet. He was either Nathaniel or Maximus. The twins were easy to pick out even if she didn't know which was which. The only difference she could see was that one was slightly darker than the other.

"She's barely a mouse. I could squash her with my boot," Kirima laughed.

"You could squash an elephant with that boot of

yours," the man sitting in a gilded chair stated.

He would be handsome if it weren't for the harsh glare he was shooting in Kirima's direction.

"How about I squash your head," Kirima snapped.

"Go ahead and try. You know the penalty of doing any harm to a pureblood."

So gilded chair was Maximus. Now that Molly studied him further, he seemed like the arrogant royal type. Entitled because of a title. She'd dealt with many men like him in her life. Jocks who'd tormented her in high school, professors who'd belittled her in college; She'd learned the hard way that being the nice girl got you nothing but footprints on your face.

"Can it, then, all of you! This is not the time for your petty bickering," one of the twins finally spoke up. It was the lighter of the two.

The Council members turned their gazes on Molly. She felt like shrinking under their intense glares, but that wouldn't help her here. She smirked and placed a hand on her hip—time to put her big girl panties on.

"All this fuss for a bunch of regular old entitled douchebags," she said and for a moment wondered if she'd gone a bit too far as they all glared at her, but then, to her surprise, they burst into laughter.

"A noisy, little mouse, this one," Kirima said.

Nathaniel turned to her with a haughty expression. "Would you expect any less from such a filthy sire?"

"Listen, I'm only here because I can only do business with other Vamps if you give the okay. So, I'm here. Yeah, I was brought back by that bitch, but trust me when I say if I ever saw her again, I'd be the first to run a stake through her heart," Molly said.

"You know that doesn't instantly kill a Vampire, right?" the twin with the darker tan asked.

"Yeah, but that doesn't make it hurt any less. Maura

deserves all the pain and suffering karma has in store," Molly replied.

"Karma? So, the rumors of your magic are true," Maximus said, shifting uncomfortably in his gilded throne.

"It's a figure of speech," Molly replied inwardly, cursing herself for slipping up.

Xander had warned her not to make any references that could be misconstrued as knowledge of magic if she wanted to avoid talking about the powers she still had yet to figure out. Her unfortunate abilities seemed the only reason Molly was being forced to endure this meeting.

"Regardless, I at least came prepared to test out this rumor."

Maximus snapped his fingers. Through the second set of doors, a young woman came in escorted by a guard. She looked frail and tired. Once she stopped in front of Molly, she could sense a strong connection with this woman. Almost like a family member, Molly was drawn to her. Without thinking, Molly started to reach out to this woman, but something stopped her. Not just something but a voice in her head. A voice she was all too familiar with, the Shadow.

Don't.

Why not?

It will make things worse.

How?

Don't ask questions. Just stand there like the idiot you are.

Molly wanted to argue with the Shadow, but deep down, she knew it was right. There was something about this girl, this woman. She felt like home. It made Molly feel like crying. Instead, she stood there and pretended like the Shadow told her to do. The first and probably last time Molly would ever do exactly as instructed by it.

"Tell me, Slave. What do you see?" Maximus commanded.

Molly really hated this guy. The woman looked up; her eyes connected with Molly's. A glazed-over stare that Molly had seen many times with the drug addicts that had passed through her life. Still, the woman didn't seem drugged. This indifference was much worse. She'd given up on life and on living. The woman was nothing more than a shell of her former self, and it made Molly want to punch something or preferably someone. She broke eye contact with the woman for just a second to glare at Mr. Entitled slaveholder. She hadn't liked the guy from the start, but now she had to remind herself of her own precarious situation to keep from lashing out.

Molly turned her attention back to the diminutive woman in front of her. She could feel the power surge within her just as the need to free this woman from whatever hell she was in wrapped itself around her heart. The woman's eyes cleared almost immediately a brief glimmer of hope before it died out again, and the woman gave an almost imperceptible shake of her head. Not for her master, but for Molly before her eyes fell to the ground once more.

"Yes, Master. There is a trace of magic within this woman but nothing of substance. Diluted so much I was only able to detect it because of my own potency," she said.

The woman's voice barely above a whisper.

"Probably residual magic from her uncouth resurrection. Be Gone," Maximus snorted.

The woman shuffled away without a single glance back at Molly. It took all of her strength not to rush forward and strangle the man who held this woman captive.

One day she will be free.

So now you are back? How do you know?

You will save me.

The woman's voice joined the mental party.

How are you in my head?

We are linked now and forever, my sister. Be safe.

Molly tried to reach out again. She willed her brain to reconnect, but something was blocking them now that the door was closed. Molly had a feeling it wasn't the physical barrier between her and the woman. All she could hope was that one day that barrier would fall again, and when it did, Molly would be ready. Molly didn't know when or how, but she would be. In the meantime, she had her own life to focus on.

"Are we done here? I have a business to run," Molly snapped

The Council members exchanged glances.

"We'll be in touch," Kirima said and gestured towards the door Molly had entered.

She turned on her heel and marched to the door. Not bothering to hide the fact that she was pissed. This entire meeting had been a giant waste of time. They hadn't asked a single question about her business, about her relationship with Maura. It seemed their only interest in her had been about her rumored powers. That was disturbing in itself, especially given the woman they'd brought in to test her.

How was it possible in this day and age for anyone to have, let alone justify, the use of slave labor for any reason? Thankfully, Molly hadn't lost control back there. She had a feeling that if she was as powerful as they'd hoped that her fate would have been worse than death. A life of servitude so bleak it robbed you of your will to live. She felt relieved and defeated at the same time. She may have been saved, but that poor woman was still living that hell.

"Let's get the fuck out of here," Molly said, marching right past Xander and to the elevators.

"That good, huh?" he asked.

Molly huffed, jamming the elevator button again and again as if it would make the damn thing show up any faster. Xander placed his hand over hers and brought it to her side. Tears were already welling in her eyes.

"Deep breaths. It's just a few minutes until we are out of here, but I need you to keep it together until we leave the building. No weakness, remember."

"Right, no weakness," she replied.

Her hands still shook like leaves in the wind.

***

Maximus exited the conference room leaving the other council members to bicker amongst themselves. The idiots were oblivious to the real issue that this meeting had presented. Despite what his slave had said, Maximus knew there was more to this Molly woman than she showed.

"Sir! Can you spare a moment?" Brody called from behind him.

Maximus scowled and turned to face the man he'd hoped would be a suitable mate for his daughter. Brody was a Vampire of action. He was ambitious and cunning. Up until recently, Maximus had no reason to doubt the man's judgment. Maximus knew all about his dalliance with Molly. After having met the woman, experiencing first hand her magnetism, it didn't surprise him. All of Maura's progeny were attractive, the perfect specimens to ensnare her prey.

Molly may be the first female Maura had turned,

but it wasn't out of character. Maura was a formidable mind. If she were born a man, there was no doubt she would have been one of the great generals in history. Unfortunately for her and for the rest of the world, she'd been born a woman. A beautiful woman at that. Her fault of intelligence landed her in the hands of a slave trader instead of a wealthy husband. That slave trader had also happened to be the number one seller of blood slaves to the Vampire elite of the time.

A series of unfortunate coincidences that created the most dangerous woman in the world. So dangerous she'd even managed to trick her own slaves into thinking she was dead and gone for years. Now she was back and forming new prodigy that matched the current era. Women were openly dating other women now so having a beautiful woman to tempt them was par for the course. In no way did it make Molly any more impressive than the rest. If anything, it made her more of a threat. Molly was evidence that not only had Maura survived her slaves' uprising, but she'd evolved. Fighting a relic with set patterns was easy. Fighting an evolving madwoman was like navigating an ever-changing maze.

"No, I have to get back home to Carolina. See to it that the proper reports are sent to my uncle," Maximus said not slowing his pace.

It was a lie. Carolina was not at home waiting for him as she should be. Carolina was locked away at a rehab facility. She'd been after Maximus for ages about having a chance to mingle with real-life Vampires. She had chosen the facility as a controlled environment, knowing Maximus would never allow her to go out into the real world. Carolina was smart, but Maximus was smarter. It was a terrible idea, but with Maura on the loose it was better she was away from the family at the moment. No matter how much Maura had evolved, one thing would never change. Maura had a taste for purebloods, and it was only a matter of time before she made her move against them once again.

Sadness so deep it chilled his bones crept over him. Maura had done so much damage already. The curse she'd placed on his family had taken more than just the life of his great, great grandfather. Every woman to mate into his family had passed of some unexplained illness. No woman had been born to their line since Maura's uprising, at least until Carolina, and Maximus lived every day in fear that she, too, would fall prey to the curse.

Many magic wielders had been put to death as retaliation for helping Maura. They were all but extinct at this point, and the few survivors were weak from lack of practice and fear. He'd managed to find a few powerful ones. Slaves that he kept to cast wards and protective spells over his household. He even forced them to feed Carolina so she may carry some magic blood to help ward off the curse if it ever came for her.

Maximus wished the rumors had been real. That Molly had stolen all of Maura's power. Then he could have killed her and ended the threat. Ended the curse on his family. Maybe she was precisely what he'd thought. There was no way for Maximus to do anything about it now. The council didn't see her as a threat even if he did. They had only agreed to this meeting because Maximus was a pureblood and could make their lives hell if they'd disagreed. They could care less about Maura and any of her progeny as long as they weren't blatantly killing other Vampires. Maximus would have to keep an eye on Molly. Even more so than the three remaining of Maura's Men.

❋❋❋

Cat had been pacing the halls of the mansion for hours. The last twenty-four hours had been nerve-racking for her. Cat wasn't even the one being forced in front of the council. Being Xander's mate, she was under his jurisdiction which meant she was just as much an outsider as he was. A social pariah, which was honestly okay with Cat. From her limited experience with other Vampires, she hadn't been all that impressed.

"So, what did they say?" Cat asked anxiously as her best friend and mate returned to the mansion.

The Council visit was a big deal. So big, that even the Shadow had made an appearance. It was the first time that it had come to Cat without mentioning Shane and Molly getting back together. The Shadow had seemed somewhat exasperated by the whole ordeal.

"Nothing really," Molly said.

Cat knew her friend better than that. It was written in the slump of her shoulders, the downcast eyes. Something was eating at her.

"Look, I get it if you don't want to go into specifics, but you are obviously not okay," Cat said.

"Catherine! The woman just met with the most powerful Vampires in the region about if her life would be spared. Give her some time to process," Xander said, pulling her into his arms.

"But..."

Xander kissed her cutting off Cat's protest. It was a desperate kiss. Xander didn't do desperate. He was the calmest most put together man Cat had ever met. It was one of the things that infuriated her the most about him and also one of the things she loved the most.

"Ugh, get a room," Molly said.

Cat pulled away from Xander just in time to see the tail end of Molly's eye roll.

"So, are you going to talk about it?"

"Cat," Xander warned.

"Stay out of it," Molly and Cat said in unison which made them both fall into a fit of laughter.

Xander threw up his hands and stormed out of the room exasperated. Cat shrugged and linked arms with her best friend. She'd smooth things over with her mate later. For now, she had something to discuss with Molly.

"So that's it? They didn't ask any questions about the club or your intentions?"

They were sitting in the movie theater eating popcorn and not watching Children of the Corn. Gretchen had joined them, but she was snoring away, obviously worn out from a night working and the sexual gymnastics she and Claude were generally partaking in whenever she was home. Cat had walked in on them several times around the house and was always on Claude to keep their forays confined to their area of the mansion like she and Xander did. Cat still refused to eat at the kitchen counter after the last incident.

"They were more worried about my powers," Molly said staring into her bowl of popcorn.

"So, did you show it to them? Were you able to?" Cat asked.

"No and no. I mean, the Council pissed me off. It was right there under the surface, but nothing came to fruition. Honestly, it's for the better. I don't think I'd be standing here now if I had. Anyway, the Council itself wasn't that bad. It was the pureblood prick that bothered me the most," Molly said.

That got Cat's attention.

"Pureblood prick have a name?"

"Maximus. He had a fucking slave Cat! Like what century are we in? How is that even possible? Like

I need the Council's approval to operate in polite Vampire society, but I sure as hell don't want anything to do with a system that condones slavery," Molly said.

"What the fuck! How did you keep your cool with a fucking slave in the room?" Cat said outraged.

"I barely held it together. If I could have done something, anything other than pretend like it didn't bother me, I would have. Even the Shadow stepped in to help me keep my shit together. Apparently, she's only down with torture if it's her torturing me," Molly said.

Cat shook her head.

"So that's it, then. They are fucking slave owning bastards who were only interested in your power," Cat said.

"Exactly," Molly said.

"Not exactly," the shadow said, appearing out of nowhere as per her style.

Both Cat and Molly jumped at her sudden intrusion.

"Can you wear like a cat bell or something? You scare the shit out of me when you do that," Cat cursed.

"Yeah, a cat bell would be nice," Molly cosigned before cringing as if the Shadow was torturing her again.

"Stop it! Say what you came to say," Cat said impatiently.

Molly unclenched her body as the Shadow eased up and whirled on Cat.

"Don't speak to me as if I'm some unwanted nuisance! Without me you would all have been dead long ago. Especially the ungrateful one. I helped her stay tethered to the gray as long as I could hoping Shane could find the spell to bring her back before Maura was able to use it," the Shadow snapped.

"So, you know how I was brought back and you didn't

think that was pertinent information for me to have," Molly said.

"Look, thank you or whatever, but forgive me. I am grateful for your help, but you aren't exactly nice about it. You pop up out of the blue to berate me or to torture my best friend. That doesn't exactly scream friendly neighborhood ghost if you know what I'm saying," Cat said.

"Fine, I will try not to berate you if you stop failing at the simple tasks I instruct you to do. Just be warned, the Council is not your friend. They must never know of Molly's power, especially not Maximus. He will seek to control her and her power. Molly has seen firsthand what he does to powerful witches. It is not a fate I would wish on my worst enemy," the Shadow said.

"Hello! I'm right here. You could speak to me directly," Molly said.

"Are you and Shane together forever as of late?"

"No," Molly grumbled.

"Then I will only help those that are worthy of my guidance," the Shadow replied.

Cat shot a perturbed look at her friend. The last thing she needed was for the Shadow to become agitated once again.

"So, the Council and Maximus are on our shit list. Got it. Anything else?" Cat asked.

"Maura is the priority. Remember that," the Shadow said before disappearing.

Gretchen stirred in her chair before stretching and yawning.

"What did I miss," She asked.

Cat and Molly exchanged glances and shook their heads.

"Just half the movie. You can go back to sleep. I'm going to need you to cover the bar again tonight," Molly said.

"If you want me well rested, don't tell Claude I'm down here if you run into him on your way out," she grumbled before curling back up to sleep.

65

REHAB

"**S**hane? Would you like to share with the group this week?"

Shane looked up from the riveting marble tiles at his feet and made eye contact with the woman across from him. Dr. Hartford, or Sharla as she liked to be called, was looking at him expectantly. He gazed slowly around the circle. Two men in teak folding chairs with their heads hung low sat at either side of Dr. Hartford. Nothing was too good for the motley crew of addicts and mentally unstable in residence. In the week since he'd arrived, he'd never seen the men look up or even speak. To Shane's left was the twitchy human who reminded Shane of his dealer back home. The man looked up and hissed revealing fake fangs. It was meant to be intimidating, the man was probably still pissed Shane had outed him for having contraband.

Shane might not have said anything if the man had offered to share. Maybe even if the price he demanded wasn't so steep. A little molly would undoubtedly have helped him get through the last week even if it wasn't his Molly of choice. The tweaky bastard had wanted him to convince Carrie to spend a night in the man's bed. That was never going to happen. Shane was far past delivering beautiful, young women to the unworthy. Shane flicked his gaze to the right and saw

Carrie smiling encouragingly at him.

Carrie was a sweet girl. She'd quickly befriended him the first week of rehab. As far as he could tell, she had absolutely no reason to be locked up here with the rest of the broken people he'd come across. Her confidence in him gave him the push he needed to finally open up. Shane opened the composition book he'd been given to write down his thoughts. The cardboard still stiff and new, barely a crease in the spine. Shane used to journal routinely in his youth, a habit that had been useful in his pursuit of science. Now, it felt odd to write things down. There was nothing about his life he honestly wanted to remember. Even the happy memories with Molly were tainted now. Shane ran his hands through his hair giving it a slight tug before letting his hand fall back to the crisp pages in his lap.

"I'll give it a try, I guess," he said.

Sharla smiled at him careful not to reveal her canines to the humans attending the night group session. The rehab facility was well known for helping out celebrities and the wealthy, so it had come as a surprise to Shane that they had an entire program to help Vampires. Well, it was mostly humans who thought they were Vampires, but a few real ones like himself and Carrie were in attendance as well. It was weird for Shane to socialize with anyone other than his friends. Being one of Maura's Men had condemned him to live even further in the shadows than being a Vampire had. Still, here he was, just the young turn of a wealthy Vampire. One who was too precious and valuable to his sire to dispose of instead of shelling out however much it took to keep his cover here at the facility.

"Red is in everything I see. Red like her curls, like the freckles on her cheeks, the subtle hue of her lips tender from my kiss. Red like her blood staining the concrete, leaking from her body. Blue like the color of her eyes, the color of her body as it lay lifeless and cold, the pills I take to numb the ache. Black like the smoke curling from my pipe, the ashes I tap from the bowl, the void I am desperate to fill, the darkness that's swallowed me whole."

Shane stopped, suddenly aware of just how much of his soul he'd just barred to these complete strangers. A few of the participants nodded their heads in queer solidarity. He was afraid to turn to his right and see the look on Carrie's face. They'd talked in depth about a multitude of things but never this. Never Molly, never the reason he'd welcomed addiction into his life like the soft blanket a child clings to in times of distress.

"Thank you, Shane. That was a good start," Sharla said before prompting for someone else to read from their journal.

At first, it seemed weird to Shane that these group sessions weren't so much a discussion as just people reading what they wrote or sharing what they drew. Now after having finally participated, he understood. Sharing with strangers without fear of judgment or reprisal was somewhat freeing. He felt a small bit of relief that he'd finally revealed a little of how he felt and hadn't been forced to apologize, explain, or analyze. He shook his head remembering how little he'd thought of his social studies colleagues at the university. Especially the psychology professors who'd tried to warn him about the possible damage his research could inflict on the participants. They'd been proven right long ago, but now he truly understood their righteous anger.

He'd sinned long before Maura's influence. He'd put people's physical and mental health at risk, and for what? A little recognition? A pat on the back? To prove to his father that life as an academic was just as admirable as life in service to one's country? The thought of his father sent Shane reaching in his pocket to where he usually kept a joint or two. Old habits that needed to die if he were going to get out of this place anytime soon. The session was over. Shane had no idea what the others had said or any memory of being dismissed. His thoughts were now occupied with avoidance. He needed some fresh air to clear his mind.

Shane did his best to push the thought of his father from his mind, but that only seemed to make it worse. It had been a long time since Shane had thought of him, and now the old man's flabby jowls shaking with rage as he puffed his ever-present cigar came to mind. That had been the night Shane had told his father was going to college instead of boot camp. His father had yelled and cursed, dashing the lovely dinner mom had made to the floor as he'd flipped the table to get to Shane faster. He'd grabbed Shane by the collar and lifted him from the air.

"You disrespectful, coward!" he'd cursed.

His vision of that night was so clear it was as if it were happening all over again, for real. Shane could feel his father's hand move from his shirt collar to his throat. The man's hands were so large that his forefinger and thumb connected at the nape of his neck. Thick fingers, rough and calloused from years of toiling in the dirt and whatever else one did as an Infantryman, tightened and squeezed like a snake until his eyes bulged and his face turned red. Shane could hear the high pitch wails of his mother as she cried and screamed, begging his father to let him go. He remembered focusing on the portraits that lined the walls. His great-great-grandfather, his great-grandfather, his grandfather, his father, and each of his three older brothers all in uniform during some point in their career, smiling like there was no other place they'd rather be. Darkness began to close in as his oxygen-starved brain began to drift away, slowly shutting down.

"Shane?"

Carrie's voice startled Shane from his hallucination. He gasped for air as reality began to register again. He was no longer in his parents' dining room about to die at the hands of his own father. He was sitting in the courtyard of the rehab facility. His journal laying open on the ground having fallen off his lap at some point, and his hands were shaking and cold. He gripped them tight to try to stay the tremors and felt the moisture between his fingers. He'd never had sweaty palms before.

"It's okay. They're just withdrawal symptoms," Carrie said, kneeling in front of him.

"Shouldn't those have passed already?"

Carrie smiled softly and shook her head.

"Depends on how long you were abusing. As Vampires, our metabolism may clear the drugs from our system quickly, but the mental effects are just as damaging as to any human," she said.

"So, you're an addict as well?"

Since they had never talked about why they were in rehab, it was interesting to finally see what cracks lie beneath her pristine surface. Carrie was a beautiful woman even by Vampire standards. Of course, it was rare that an unattractive woman was ever turned. She was what people in his day would call a fox. Farrah Fawcett would be put to shame next to her blue eyes and cheerful grin. Shane hoped her addictions weren't because of an unwanted turning by a sadistic sire. Granted, since she was here, that wasn't a likely scenario. Shane was probably imprinting his own experience on her. Either way, unattached female

Vampires, while becoming more plentiful, were still relatively rare. Even amongst the born Vampires, the birth rates were 5 to 1 in favor of a male child. At least from what information Shane had been able to gather on his two short trips to the Vampire archives.

That trip had been the only pleasurable experience he'd had under Maura's tutelage. She'd wanted to check the lineage of a specific Vampire and of course hadn't been able to risk being seen there herself. The sheer volume of knowledge had been overwhelming. So many secrets, so much history both lost and unknown to that of humankind. It had been a small slice of heaven in the midst of his own personal hell. It had been that outing that had allowed Shane, Xander, and Claude to come up with their plan to defeat Maura. Those blissful moments where they were temporarily free from the deep thrall she typically held over them.

He shook his head. He was drifting off into the crevices of his psyche again instead of focusing on what was right in front of him. He could claim it was a side effect of his drug use but in reality, he'd always been that way. Countless teachers had scolded him for spending more time in his own head than in reality itself.

"No, I'm not a substance abuser. Unless you count coffee. It makes me feel more human to drink it," Carrie said blushing and tucking her chin in.

It was a cute gesture typical of a young child, not a woman of her age. She had to be in her twenties at least at turning. Perhaps it was not drugs but some other mental disorder that she needed help with. That didn't make sense either. She seemed perfectly able when she spoke with him earlier in the week. The more Shane got to know Carrie the bigger the mystery she became, and if Shane liked anything, it was solving a good mystery.

Shane didn't have a chance to question her further as one of the orderlies came out and reminded them of their curfew. Carrie continued to blush as she turned and walked away towards the women's dormitory. With a sigh and an anxious glance at the intrusive orderly, he picked up his discarded journal and made his way to his own room.

❋❋❋

"Such an idiot!" Carrie cursed herself once she was safely in her room.

She flopped down on the bed that was barely more than a cot in comparison to her luxurious four-poster bed at home. In fact, this entire set up was a significant downgrade from where she could be staying, at least in appointments. The whole room was smaller than her shoe closet. Gosh what she wouldn't give for access to her wardrobe right now. If she had her personal closet at her disposal, Shane wouldn't stand a chance. He'd take one look at her and fall instantly at her feet. Except maybe not. He was one of Maura's Men after all.

When Carrie felt the dark presence within him, she'd been shocked. She'd grown up hearing tales of Maura's Men. Reckless Dandies and Dark Warriors who'd sold their souls to the devil for a chance at immortality. Handsome men with black souls who feasted on the hearts of young women alongside Maura. She'd been drawn to him immediately. Curious at first to see if the rumors were true. Then she'd gotten to know him. He was definitely not soulless. He had depth, so much depth, and so much pain. His spirit was broken and not just by Maura. After his poem today she knew he was, in fact, capable of love, and she was so drawn to him. She wanted to save him in whatever way she could.

At least before her father forced her home to mate his choice.

She wanted Shane to be her choice, but she knew that could never be. No way would her father allow her to be tainted by one of Maura's Men. The family would fall in disgrace. Thinking of home always made her sad. She loved her rooms, loved the gardens. She missed the staff who were more family than her blooded relatives in some respects. Except home was just as much a prison as this place. The only benefit was not dealing with the pressures of being a born Vampire. As many luxuries as it offered, it was still just a gilded cage.

No, she would enjoy this break as much as she could. She would pursue Shane while she could and make the best of her limited freedom while she still could. Carrie closed her eyes and thought about Shane's gaunt features, using her mind to fill them in and give them life. She imagined herself sprawled on a bed, naked and open for him, not just her body but her vein. How would his canines feel piercing the tender flesh of her neck? Better yet the sensitive bud between her lower lips?

Carrie slid her hand down her body to touch herself right where it ached. She'd seen human women in movies do these things, but had never done so herself. Never felt the need to, until now. Imagining Shane feeding on her, taking strength from her. Blood sharing between Vampires was a very intimate experience and wasn't done lightly, but she could see giving Shane part of her. Becoming part of him, forever. She was hesitant as her hand slid past the elastic band of her sweatpants, pausing at the edge of her lace underwear.

She knew no one was watching, but she looked around the room just to be sure. Stopping to pull the thin blanket over her body just in case. She started her descent once again. This time slightly less hesitant. Her imagination taking the reins. Carrie was right at the source, her hand hovering over the moist flesh that was begging for some sort of release from the throbbing arousal coursing through her.

Ring! Ring! Ring! Ring!

Carrie nearly jumped out of her skin. Of course, how had she forgotten about her father's weekly call?

"Have you come to your senses yet," he asked right away.

Maximus was never one to beat around the bush. So much so that he insisted on going by a single name. He had no room for titles or the undue flattery that came along with them. Most people saw him as a harsh man, and he could be, but Carrie knew his one soft spot. That soft spot was her. Carrie was his only weakness, and as such, he was suffocating in his worry and need to protect her. Especially after the death of her mother.

She'd contracted a mysterious illness shortly after her fourth birthday. Carrie was young, and her father had tried to shield her from the details, but she knew it had been a painful death. She still remembered the way the staff and scurried around doing their best to make noise as they moved around her room, in a failed effort to drown out her mother's wailing cries. There had been rumors of witchcraft, of a curse placed on her family by Maura.

"Have you come to yours?"

"Carolina, my sweet daughter. I thought we'd already made it past the rebellious stage. Please, just come home."

Maximus was trying a different tactic. He'd tried it before, and it hadn't worked then any more than it would work now. Carrie had made up her mind. If she was ever going to be more than just some royal trophy wife, she needed to establish a level of independence from her father.

"I am no longer a child that you can easily manipulate. Have a good evening, father, and please don't berate the staff too much in your anger for not getting your way," Carrie said and hung up the phone.

She tried to come back to her thoughts of Shane, but talking to her father had truly ruined the mood. Instead, she snuggled tighter into her blanket and closed her eyes. Mentally planning her approach to seducing Shane. One thing she would take from her father would be his mind for manipulation. She would help Shane become the man she knew he could be. Then he would have no choice but to see her as the only woman meant to be with him.

QUESTIONS

"**Y**our friends are meeting without you. That doesn't bode well for our plans," Rachel stated, startling Cat from her chair. You would think the woman would be used to her surprise visits by now.

"I have a deadline to meet, and I seriously don't have time for your drama right now," Cat replied taking her seat and ignoring Rachel.

"You aren't taking this seriously enough!" Rachel lost her temper for what seemed the hundredth time.

Cat glared back at her over what the woman called a laptop. There was much about the modern world that still puzzled Rachel. She'd missed a lot while trapped in the gray plotting her revenge on Maura. It wasn't until Molly's resurrection that she'd been allowed access to the present. A necessary tool to seek her revenge and restore balance.

Before then Rachel had all but faded away, stewing in the grief and anger of Xander's betrayal. She'd almost given up on reaching the light. She'd seen it a few times in the distance but had never been able to reach it herself. No, she had been stuck in the quicksand of gray until that fateful day when the balance of life and death had been destroyed.

By bringing Molly back using her dark magic, Maura

had torn a hole in the boundaries between the world of the living and the dead. A hole that it was Rachel's job to fix. A task that would finally bring her salvation, her trip into the light, and the key to her final peace.

She'd been woken and given the knowledge needed to bring about the demise of Maura for her infractions against the laws of nature. Still, she couldn't do it all on her own. She needed the help of this maddening woman to complete her goal.

"I'm not even going to respond to that nonsense," Cat said coolly.

Rachel wished so badly to be able to interact with Cat in the same way she could with Molly. Instead, Rachel did the only thing she could.

"Your sloth will be the death of everyone and everything you hold dear," she stated and disappeared from the room.

Still, Rachel didn't leave the realm of the living. She had one more stop to make before she returned to the gray.

One benefit of moving in shadow form was the element of stealth. No one saw her enter Greg's room, nor did he stir when she lay her form next to his on the bed. Rachel marveled at the sleeping male before her, lingering longer in this realm than she should just for a minute of peace with him. She could feel what little life she had left draining faster with every second she was away from the gray.

Rachel had no business coveting this man. No, she was only here to seek revenge on Maura and save her soul from the gray. Whatever fantasies she had about Greg, none of them would ever be. She was a ghost, a shadow just waiting for the light to come and take her. Her destiny was death, not life and love.

Greg stirred and smiled at her. Rachel smiled back.

"Don't go," he pleaded as she faded away.

As much as she wanted to stay, there was too much pulling her away.

❈❈❈

Molly sat at her desk staring blankly at the documents in front of her. Tan pieces of parchment deceptively fragile in her hands. There was a weight to them, so heavy it seemed a brick wall had been placed on her chest. The Council's decree that she bends to their will was the last thing she needed to add to her already ill-fated existence. At least they had conditionally lifted the ban on her establishment. Not that it was entirely unexpected. As soon as she'd met them it was clear they could care less about her business dealings. They were more afraid of her mysterious power. She'd done her best to hide it from them. Even the poor woman who tested her had covered for her. Yet she had a feeling it still hadn't been enough to satisfy them that she wasn't a threat.

Her so-called power. A magical weapon she had no idea how to use or control. A curse she hadn't known she had until that awful night. A light so intense it had stopped whatever evil spell Maura had cast upon Claude and Gretchen. Well, at least mostly. It hadn't been enough to destroy Maura. That crazy hag was still out there somewhere. No doubt planning her next attack. This time with Molly as her number one target. A knock sounded on Molly's office door.

"Come in," she called shoving the parchment under a stack of vendor orders.

Gretchen peeked her head in, a bright smile on her face.

"Are you busy?" she asked pleasantly.

Molly pasted on a smile. Even though Gretchen was

now a close friend, Molly didn't want to burden the girl with her news. Gretchen had quite a bit to deal with on her own, having given up most of her family and nearly losing her brother and Claude to Maura. Molly envied the girl's ability to cope. Although it probably had a lot to do with the fact that since his recovery, Claude had barely gone a few hours without stealing her away to a locked room or dark corner.

A sharp pang of jealousy jolted her chest. An unwanted sentiment. Molly was done with love. It had literally gotten her killed, and after the disastrous affair with Brody, Molly knew now that even carefully constructed flings were not much better. It seemed Molly's love life was doomed to casual flirtations and battery-operated boyfriends. Suddenly realizing she'd yet to answer Gretchen, Molly cleared her throat and nodded.

"Just a bit. The bar is in disarray after you and Mack both taking a vacation and me being distracted with Council business."

"Right. The Council," Gretchen said with a shiver, "Sorry, I guess now wouldn't be the best time for an ice cream break."

Molly laughed.

"Probably not, but I could really use a pleasant distraction at the moment," Molly cringed slightly at her revelation.

She wasn't handling things all that well, but Gretchen didn't need to know that. Thankfully, Gretchen didn't so much as raise an eyebrow. Unlike Cat, Gretchen tended to be a bit more diplomatic about other people's privacy. If Gretchen was suggesting an ice cream break, something was bothering her as well.

After their first ice cream outing, Claude had installed an ice cream parlor in the mansion. His way of ensuring that Gretchen had no excuse to leave his side longer than he deemed necessary. He hadn't liked the idea of her being out in public without him. Of the three men, well four that now lived in the mansion, Claude was the most demanding when it came to protecting his conquests. Not that Gretchen was a pushover by any means.

"What's on your mind," Molly asked.

Gretchen twirled her spoon in the half-eaten banana split. Despite not being able to taste the flavor as strongly as before, Gretchen usually savored every bite until her treat was gone. Being sired by Maura, the men were shunned from Vampire society, making their knowledge of the culture limited. Molly, having been accepted into regular Vampire society until recently, had been able to learn a lot more than they ever could. This made Molly a walking encyclopedia for Cat and Gretchen's curiosities. Gretchen set her spoon aside and crossed her arms over her chest.

"Can Vampires have children?" Gretchen asked.

Molly nearly choked on her mouthful of ice cream.

"Excuse me," she gasped.

"Just a question. I mean, I'm not planning to— Is it even an option?" Gretchen mumbled.

"As far as I know only purebloods can actually birth a child. Turned Vampires only have children in the creepy I killed you then brought you back to life with my blood way," Molly said.

❈❈❈

"You know, I'm starting to feel a little left out," Cat said plunking herself into the booth next to Molly.

She grabbed the spoon from her best friend and stole a bite from her sundae. Gretchen blushed obviously embarrassed. The girl was so sensitive it reminded Cat of Molly in the old days. Before she'd become a bitter, old shrew. Molly snatched her spoon back and glared at Cat.

"Did your mate send you to spy?" Molly quipped.

Cat laughed. If only Xander gave her that much credit. No, her mate had no idea she had even left the confines of the fortress they called home. Despite having built them an ice cream bar at the mansion, sometimes a girl just needed a bit of fresh air, a change of scenery. Truly, Cat loved that Xander was protective of her. It was something Cat had rarely experienced in her human life. Being a strong, confident, independent woman, she was often in conflict with it.

"Actually, it was our dear shadow friend," Cat said instantly shutting her friend up.

The Shadow hadn't exactly been kind to Molly, and God knew it was probably the only thing left in the world that actually scared her more then finally giving in to her love for Shane.

"What demands has it made now," Molly sighed before handing Cat a second spoon.

"Oh, the usual, get Molly and Shane together or suffer the consequences. Honestly, I'm getting a little annoyed with being her mouthpiece," Cat said.

She dug into the sundae. Not that it tasted like anything, but Cat could still enjoy the cool sensation it left as it slid down her throat.

"At least it's better than having it torture you at random."

Molly rubbed her arms as if she were cold despite it being a pleasant temperature in their favorite ice cream parlor. A funny reaction considering the Shadow had a habit of using heat and flame to scare the not so living daylights out of her.

"Or having it slink around your brother," Gretchen

muttered under her breath.

Now that caught Cat's attention. This was an incredible new piece of information. There was no telling whether the Shadow was female or not, but over the time Cat had spent in the Shadow's presence, she had a vague idea of who or what the Shadow was.

"What do you mean," She asked.

Gretchen rolled her eyes.

"I've caught him in mid-conversation with the Shadow a few times, and I always get the sense that I'm intruding on some kind of intimate moment. It's super creepy to think of my brother with anyone, let alone a shadow figure with ulterior motives."

Cat exchanged glances with Molly before bursting into a fit of laughter. Not that the situation was funny in the least, but it was a better reaction to the weirdness in their lives than any alternative one.

"Well at least you know you won't have any half shadow nieces or nephews running around," Molly said.

"Wait, what did I miss? Were you asking about the possibility of children?" Cat asked Gretchen, and there was that crimson flush of her cheeks again.

The poor girl still wasn't used to Cat's directness after all the time they'd spent together.

"It was an important question. I honestly couldn't handle any more life-changing surprises in my relationship with Claude. That man is enough to handle as it is," she said, fussing with the ever-present scarf around her neck.

Cat did her best not to stare as the scarf slipped slightly out of place. A jagged raised scar marred her otherwise flawless skin. It looked like she'd been mauled by a bear. Gretchen saw it as a reminder of her weakness. Cat saw it as sign of her strength. She'd fought Declan hard as a human could, giving enough time for Claude to save her. That didn't mean she was a damsel in distress. Gretchen had killed Declan herself for what he did to her. Cat nodded in acknowledgment of her friend's statement and to clear her own head.

"Yeah, and I thought Xander was bad with his whole protector of the innocent thing. Anyway, I could have answered that one for you. I mean, Xander and I have been going at it for years. Nothing has resulted from it. Well, that and it's pretty common sense that if you aren't bleeding, you aren't breeding."

"Oh geez, could you be crasser?" Molly asked.

Cat was just about to reply when a group of young men approached their table.

"Mind if we join you?" one of the men asked.

Cat wiggled her eyebrows at Molly before turning to say yes, but before she could answer Xander and Claude were there, pushing themselves into the booth.

"Seats taken," Claude bit out before pulling Gretchen into a kiss so passionate it was X-rated.

Xander being much more mindful of appearances draped an arm over Cat's shoulder and pulled her in close. That left Molly as the odd woman out, but the look Xander shot the boys had them all scattering to the winds. Now alone, Cat turned to Xander, fire in her eyes.

"Are you having me followed?" she spat.

Xander grinned before giving Cat a quick peck.

"Only when you sneak out," he said a glint of challenge in his eyes.

If Cat wasn't so madly in love with her mate, she'd have smacked the smug grin off his face. Instead, she kissed him. Reaching over him she lifted the car keys from his jacket pocket before pushing him out of the booth.

"Time to go home so I can punish you properly," she said.

"Ugh! All of you just go before we're all kicked out for indecency," Molly grumbled.

Cat flicked her off before pushing Xander towards the door. Someday soon, Cat was going to have a real come to Jesus talk with her bestie. For now, she had more pressing needs. Needs that involved complete privacy and the dead sexy warrior in front of her.

RED FLAG

"**I** thought they would never leave," Brody said sliding into the booth across from Molly.

Molly glared at him and silently kicked herself for deciding to stay to finish her sundae instead of going home.

"What do you want?"

Molly set he spoon down and crossed her arms over her chest.

"To spend time with you," he answered.

Molly signaled for the check.

"Look we had a thing. It's over now. Leave me alone," Molly replied.

"Is it because of that boy? I understand he was the reason you wanted to be turned in the first place, but you can't honestly tell me you're attracted to that bag of bones," Brody said with a roll of his eyes.

Molly saw red. Her power began to rise to the surface. She was already on edge because of the Council, and this was just one more thing to prick her nerves.

"Don't you dare speak about Shane that way! He is more of a man than you could ever be," she snapped.

"You're fucking delusional. If you had any sense, you'd be all over me right now. I'm rich. I have status and connections in the Vampire community. I'm the closest to pureblood that a bitch like you will ever get.

Especially with your attitude," Brody said.

His nostrils flared with anger. That made Molly feel better and helped her calm down. This was about his ego and not about her at all. If she were begging for his dick, he'd definitely give it to her, but nothing else. He got off on power. She recognized it in him the same as she'd seen in Maura during her brief time under Maura's influence.

"You're nothing more than an errand boy," Molly said coolly.

She could still feel her powers there under the surface. Worse, she saw the shock and fear in Brody's eyes. That could only mean he either saw or sensed it too. She silently cursed the slip. He could easily run to the Council and revoke his recommendation. He was an ass, but in a way, she still needed him. In that way at least.

"You'll regret this," he muttered and took off before the check was even delivered by the teenage waitress.

Molly paid the bill and left the ice cream parlor with her head held high and her spirits somewhat lifted. She may have made a mistake that would get back to the Council, but she would worry about that later. If she were to rate her boss bitch level, Molly wagered she'd be about an eight right now. Brody was a pissant. She was done with him. Molly had more important things to do than worry about a fuck boy like him. She had a business to run, a monster to hunt, and a real man to wait for.

✵✵✵

This spying shit was getting on his last nerve. Watching all these so-called traitor's live everyday lives while he was stuck being an errand boy for that maniacal bitch Maura. Rodney watched as Molly strode out of the ice cream parlor after telling off that jerk wad Council liaison. He should follow her, but he was fed up with the Queen Bee of boring shit. So instead, Rod took off in the direction of the Council's flunky. Maybe he would have better luck with intel on that front. Rod followed the greasy schmuck around the corner to where his car was parked. Rodney was just about to turn around because he wasn't about to waste time chasing a vehicle when the man's phone rang.

"Yes, sir."

Rod found a spot to hide that still allowed him to listen in as long as the guy didn't get in his blacked-out sedan.

"No, there is no sign of contact with Maura."

"I'm sure."

"Sir? I think the tests were wrong."

"Yes, I'm sure. I saw it with my own eyes. Molly is dangerous."

"Right away sir."

The man hung up and slid into his car. Rod sank further into the dark as the car's headlights flashed on in his direction. This couldn't be good. Maura wouldn't like this development one bit, but at least Rod didn't have to worry too much about her taking out her frustrations on him. He was the smartest one in her army. He controlled her accounts and made sure the ship ran undetected by local law enforcement. At least as much as possible considering the body count she racked up on a daily basis at this point.

Speaking of, Rodney doubled back to the ice cream parlor. That cute, little waitress was just the snack to appease the bitch after he dropped the bombshell he'd just uncovered. Rodney sent a text to Billy who should be out scouting in the area anyway. He was the perfect bait for this feeder fish. It didn't take long for the guy to show up and convince the teenager to take a break out back.

Billy lured the girl into the alley with promises of sweet kisses and more. Rodney had already disabled the security camera by the back door. As soon as she was out of sight of the crowded streets, Rod stepped in. Slipping behind the girl with a rag of chloroform. She was out like a light in a second and in the trunk of his car in no time. Poor thing didn't know the hell that was in store for her. Rodney would feel bad, but he'd become immune to it all. He stepped on the gas as he headed into the warehouse district. The chloroform wouldn't keep her knocked out for long, and Maura preferred her pound of flesh tender and untouched.

❀❀❀

Molly sat reading a sappy romance novel and cursing at the hapless main character.

"Fuck him! You deserve better!"

She tossed the book down and picked up the next in the series. She hated that she couldn't even enjoy books like she used too. All because of Shane. She'd let herself believe just for a moment that they could actually go back to the happy naïve couple they used to be. It was easy to let it go when the Council was her primary concern. Now after weeks of being alone and after the encounter with Brody, Molly was getting antsy.

Molly was lonely and for what? There was no guarantee that Shane would make a recovery. That he would still want her when or if he did. She'd tried distracting herself with movies and books. The problem was every wistful sigh and longing look only brought up memories of the past. Memories, both happy and painful.

"Good golly, Ms. Molly! You look positively

scrumptious this fine evening," Shane said, his gaze traveling over her appreciatively.

She'd worn an emerald green sweater to highlight her red curls and the blood red lipstick on her lips along with blue jeans to accentuate her hips and gold heels to lengthen her legs. She was short, but she knew how to make her legs look like they went all the way to heaven. It was their fourth date, and she had no idea where they were going.

"Thank you. You look quite handsome yourself," Molly blushed under his clear approval.

Shane held out his hand. Molly took it. Her heart fluttering already with just the light brush of his fingers across her palm before his hand encircled hers. He guided her down the stairs and helped her into his van. They made small talk as he drove towards the center of town.

"Where are we going," Molly asked.

They'd parked in the center of town but had already walked several blocks.

"It's a surprise. I promise it's not far. I wouldn't want you to have sore feet at the end of our date," Shane said.

He'd noticed her choice in shoes. He actually cared to note her choice and accommodate for them. If he got any sweeter Molly for sure would be a goner.

"No worries of that. The way you've swept me off my feet, I'll be on cloud nine all night," she rambled before she could catch herself.

He grinned and pulled her closer, sliding his arm around her waist.

"Is that so?" he asked with a silly grin.

It wasn't cocky but playful. Molly blushed again.

"I'm sorry. That was too much," Molly said.

"Don't be sorry. I like that you speak your truth.

Never stop doing that. Always speak your truth around me and feel safe in the knowledge that I will do the same," Shane said.

Molly looked up at him and found him gazing back at her. They stopped for a moment, and Molly was struck by a sudden realization. It had only been a month or so since their first meeting, but somehow, she'd already fallen madly in love with Shane. Sure, he was quirky and a little old-fashioned. Stuck in the seventies to be more precise but he was intelligent and worldly. She bit her lip feeling silly for just standing there staring into his hypnotizing eyes.

"Kiss me," she heard herself whisper, and he did just that.

They made out like teenagers without a care in the world before rude catcalls forced them back to reality. They broke apart in a fit of giggles.

"We should get going before it gets too crowded," Shane said, guiding her along once again.

"Where are we..." She didn't finish her sentence as she realized they were at the gates of the carnival.

She'd forgotten that the carnival was still running at this time of year. She smiled. It had been years since she'd been.

"I hope you like it," Shane said, and she nodded.

"It's perfect. You're perfect!"

Molly groaned, tossing her book aside before grabbing the TV remote and turning on the news. The news was depressing and anything but romantic, the perfect distraction from her thoughts. At least until it showed a screen full of young female faces.

Tonight's heartbreaking story, thirty young women either missing or dead. Is there a serial killer on the loose? Should a curfew be instated?

Molly recognized one of the faces as the young

waitress from the ice cream parlor and turned off the TV. If there was anything she wanted to think about less than Shane, it was the fact that Maura was still out there pillaging the innocent. Her reign of terror needed to end and soon. Not only to save the poor souls of the town but also because her shit was not good for business. A curfew would kill her club. Club Obelisk was only just barely out of the red as it was.

Molly decided to call Xander and see if there was any update on the hunt. Hopefully, she wouldn't be interrupting anything between him and Cat, but this couldn't wait. Racking up that kind of numbers, he had to have some sort of lead by now. Maybe joining the boys in their hunt for Maura would help Molly pass the time before Shane's return. Give her something else to focus on besides her growing need to have him nearby. Even if they could never go back to how things were, Molly realized she still wanted Shane in her life. They'd been good friends before, at the very least they could return to that. Even as the thought crossed her mind, Molly knew that wasn't entirely true. While being friends would be tolerable, it wasn't what her heart truly wanted.

❈❈❈

Shane sat stiffly in the leather chair across from Dr. Hartford. He wished he could stare at something other than the dull gray walls surrounding them as she went on her usual opening spiel. He was doing well in a group but had yet to open up in their private sessions. She hoped to change that soon.

"Shane, are you still with me?"

Apparently, he had missed a verbal cue.

"Sorry, I'm just a little tired," Shane said refocusing on the woman in front of him.

Dr. Hartford smiled, although it didn't reach her eyes.

"I've received reports of you spending time with Carrie. You know relationships are frowned upon during treatment," Dr. Hartford said.

"She is just a friend. A friendly face in my otherwise lonely existence here. None of the others are very keen to speak to me outside of the group," he replied.

"Does that bother you? The loneliness?"

"It doesn't bother me. I could care less about making friends. It's just nice to be seen and appreciated for who I am and not my reputation and shortcomings," Shane answered.

"You have spoken about your reputation before. Do you care to elaborate?"

"Not particularly," Shane said.

"You have made great progress here physically, Shane, but mentally you need to open up. If you aren't ready to share what is actually troubling you that's fine, but it will make your time here much more effective if you do," Dr. Hartford said.

"I have told you about my failure in relationships," Shane protested, getting frustrated with this already.

"You have told me about the girl, and while tragic, she is not the source of your troubles. There is something deeper that you haven't shared yet that has led to your poor choices in life. The lack of confidence that led you down the path towards addiction," Dr. Hartford said.

She looked down at her notes and began flipping through them.

"Last week you briefly mentioned your relationship with your human family wasn't the best. Why don't we start there?"

"I don't need to talk about that. We both know that our human lives cease to exist the moment we are turned," Shane did his best not to show his unease about the topic.

Even in his human life, he avoided talking about his family. Ever since the night his father had nearly killed him, Shane considered himself an orphan.

"That may be true, but it doesn't mean those memories don't impact our new existence. Turning doesn't wipe the slate clean as much as we may like it to," Dr. Hartford said.

"I am well aware, but my family is a non-issue," Shane snapped.

"Are you sure? You mentioned several times over the last few weeks that you feel you are a disappointment to your father. You used the present tense multiple times in that regard."

"What does it matter? The man is long dead and good riddance!"

Shane hated that he was being grilled about that man. He gripped the edge of the chair to keep from lashing out at the woman. Dr. Hartford meant well. She thought she was helping him, but at the moment, his baser instinct was in attack mode. Dr. Hartford sensed his anger and sat back in her chair. Her eyes darkening the way Vampires' eyes did when they detected a threat.

They sat for a moment, tensions steadily rising between them. Shane closed his eyes and lowered his head. It was a maneuver he'd quickly learned in situations like these. Well before he even met Maura. Maybe, Dr. Hartford was right. Perhaps Shane should open up the chapter of his life he thought was long passed. What did he have to lose at this point? Shane had already lost the trust of his friends, the love of his woman, and his dignity as a man in his quest for self-destruction. Shane released a heavy sigh before rubbing his hands over his face.

"My father was a military man, as was his father, and his father, and his father before him," Shane began.

He told the whole sordid story of his life before Maura. Of growing up the runt of the family. Always different and separate from those who were supposed to love and care for him. At the end of his story, he was exhausted both emotionally and physically, but somehow the burden he hadn't known he'd been carrying lifted from his shoulders. He'd never felt this kind of relief before, not even when they'd sealed Maura's remains at MacDonald Estate.

"I think that is enough for the evening. This was a big breakthrough for you, Shane. Just remember that therapy should be your focus here. You have to build yourself up before you can even think about sharing yourself with another person so intimately," Dr. Hartford said.

Shane chose not to acknowledge Dr. Hartford's statement. He stood with a nod and left her office, heading straight for the courtyard. He knew Carrie would be there waiting for him, and he needed a friendly face after that torturous session. Dr. Hartford was right about one thing though. He did need to focus on getting himself together. From then on, he would take his time in therapy more seriously. If not for himself, for Molly. She deserved a better man than he had been before, and with the help of Carrie and Dr. Hartford, he knew he could become that man.

SHANE'S RETURN

Shane watched from the corner as Molly smiled and laughed with the man beside her. It took all his willpower not to storm over and drag her away from him. He may not be under the influence, but the primal urges towards her were still there. Everything inside of him screamed that she was his. This was not how Shane had expected the night to go. No, in his head it had gone much differently. In his head, Molly would have seen him enter immediately, recognized that he'd changed. That he wasn't the broken man she'd come to hate but the man she loved. The man he used to be or perhaps a better version. One that was stronger and more determined than ever to have her back.

Not that he thought she would run to him and confess her undying love. That wasn't in the realm of logical, but he had at least thought he would get some acknowledgment. He hadn't expected that his grand entrance back into her life would be less than a fleeting glance in his direction. Shane sulked over to the bar not surprised that Mack greeted him with coke as soon as he arrived.

"Not what you expected, but I promise you she isn't unaware of your presence."

"Aware but indifferent," Shane sighed downing the coke and wishing it was something with more kick, but as a recovering addict he quickly banished the thought.

It was bad enough being at the bar surrounded by intoxicants and the intoxicated, but his life goals were worth more to him than the empty escape of his addictions.

"You shouldn't be here," a soft feminine voice said from behind him. He slowly turned on the bar stool to face Carrie.

"And neither should you," he said his eyes taking in his newest friend.

Carrie had been the only Vampire he'd ever met not afraid of him as one of Maura's Men. He had been genuinely happy to become friends with her, and she had been instrumental in helping him pull through to become the man he was now.

"Come on Romeo. Obviously, tonight isn't going your way. How about we blow this den of iniquity and have some real fun," she said and pulled him off the stool.

Shane could have resisted, but after glancing in Molly's direction and seeing her leading her friend to her office, well, Shane wouldn't be able to keep his cool if he stayed any longer.

"What did you have in mind?" Shane asked as they cleared the front door.

"Let's play human," she said pulling him down the street towards the restaurant district. Shane smirked.

Even locked in the confines of rehab and recovery, Carrie wanted to maintain her humanity as she liked to call it. It was a sentiment Shane was fond of. With so much crazy surrounding his life at the moment, it was good to forget his woes in a more innocent fashion.

❋❋❋

Shane was back. Of course, Molly already knew he was back. Cat had been counting the days until his return and keeping Molly painfully aware of his itinerary and how well he'd been doing in his treatment. Still, seeing him again. Seeing him not just back to his old self but somehow better. He was no longer the frail shell of a man who'd stalked her like the Crypt Keeper of failed romance. He'd filled out, his once emaciated and pale arms were bulging with muscle under tanned skin. His cheekbones no longer cut sharp, imposing shadows on his face but rather drew you from his full, pink lips to the sultry depths of his brown eyes.

Molly sank further down into her desk chair with a sigh. Her hands sliding down her thighs in an effort to push her arousal away. It was insane. She didn't have time for this. Didn't have the space left in her life to entertain the thoughts circling in her head. She needed to focus on making sure she maintained what little status she had left with the Council. Yet the more she tried to push the thoughts away, the clearer and more intrusive they came.

Molly had planned to go visit Shane at the mansion once her shift was over. Had assumed he would stay close to home upon his return. Still, Molly wasn't at all surprised that he'd come straight to her club, straight to see her. Not with the way he'd acted before. That familiar bloom of romance filled her heart as she stood and headed for the door. He'd come for her, a little late but better late than never.

When Molly returned to the front of the house, Shane was nowhere to be seen. She should have gone to him sooner. Molly hadn't really needed to continue chatting with the new Council liaison that had come to check in on her. He'd been more interested in getting her number than ensuring she was complying with the Council's edicts.

As if Molly would make that mistake again. No more Council flunkies for her. Hell, no one could ever replace Shane. It had taken time and separation for her to realize it, but she finally had. Now that Shane was back, she would make sure he knew it too. Maybe he'd taken her hesitation earlier as dismissal, as a sign that she hadn't been ready. Honestly, Molly didn't even know if she was prepared to fully forgive him, but the feeling in her heart and between her legs didn't care at that moment. She nodded at Mack before heading out the door. She was just rounding the corner when she spotted him, or rather them.

Molly saw them walking away from the club, arms linked and genuine smiles on their faces as they gazed into each other's eyes. She quickly ducked into the alleyway to avoid being seen. He hadn't come for her after all. That thought brought Molly to her knees as once again heartache ripped through her. Her pain quickly turning back into anger so intense and damningly familiar. She never thought she'd ever reach that level of fury a second time. The same burning rage that had allowed her to be manipulated by Maura into torturing her own best friend.

Molly gasped for air as the flames of her anger engulfed her, blinding white light filling her vision. She couldn't feel anything else but somehow was aware of everything around her. The brick wall next to her popping and cracking under the extreme heat that she was exuding, the smell of asphalt hot and bubbling beneath her feet. Then suddenly a vision of Mack walking towards her. His mouth was moving, but she couldn't make out the words as his hands reached out to her, beckoning her to him.

Molly shook her head unsure if she was hallucinating or not. She hoped she was because if she wasn't, Mack was in grave danger, and he was stupid to put himself in harm's way. Molly couldn't control what was happening to her, couldn't make it stop. Mostly because she didn't want to. She was tired of holding it all in. Tired of being afraid of being made to feel ashamed for things out of her control. She succumbed to the rage letting it all out into the blinding white light that she now realized was coming from her, emanating from her pores.

She closed her eyes and just when she thought it would all be over, just when the rage she was projecting began to turn in on her she felt a hand on her shoulder. That small contact was like a bucket of water over her head. Her eyes flew open as she gasped for air. The light slowly faded away as she huddled shivering in the dark alley behind the club. Mack stood over her looking both concerned and relieved.

"I think it's time you and I had a little chat," Mack said pulling Molly to her feet.

He draped his coat over her shivering frame, but instead of taking her back into the club he guided her to his car. Molly got into the beat-up, old SUV and turned out the window. She had no idea what to talk about. Her mind was completely blank as if everything but what just happened, was entirely inconsequential. Mack didn't seem to mind the silence as he drove. It was like he sensed she needed a moment to pull herself together before anything more could be accomplished.

❋❋❋

Molly studied Mack's car. The exterior was covered in dents and scratches that were only partially obscured by the peeling and faded paint job. Yet the inside was immaculate, not a crumb, a wrapper, or a receipt could be found anywhere. The only thing that gave any hint to his personal life was the weird signet ring that hung from his keychain. It swung back in forth with the motion of the car every time they stopped at a stop sign or light. It was hypnotizing to watch.

Molly had seen the ring many times before, but this was the closest she'd ever been to it. Mack was a secretive person which was okay with Molly. She understood the need for one's privacy, but now, she just needed a distraction. Any kind of diversion from her thoughts. The ring looked to be made out of bronze, the design swirled and looped in a way that hinted at Latin, Celtic, and maybe Arabic influence. Molly was no expert. She could only guess at its origins or even its meaning. For all she knew, it was something he'd gotten from one of those prize machines where you put in a quarter and got some little trinket. It seemed a bit too sturdy for that. Maybe Mack was into cosplay and the ring was a replica from some comic book or video game character.

As it swung, Molly could only catch snippets of detail, but her mind seemed to have no trouble at all filling it in. Like the symbol was one she had seen before, a long time ago. That made the most sense as to why the design seemed so familiar. After years of Cat dragging her to comic conventions, something should have stuck. A brief flash of memory slid past her conscious thought process. A shadow of a woman standing regally before her. A pitying scowl on the woman's face before a shimmering purple door slammed between them. It didn't register as anything she'd seen at the conventions but something older, from before Cat. Maybe even before becoming a foster child. It was strange indeed. Perhaps Molly's powers were just mini seizures each episode bringing her closer and closer to madness. She shivered, wondering if that is what made Maura the madwoman she was today.

"We're here," Mack announced, breaking Molly's concentration.

She looked up to find them parked in front of her

condo. She turned to ask Mack why he'd brought her home, but he was already out of the car and walking around to the passenger side.

"What if I don't want to talk?" Molly asked as they walked to her front door.

"Whether you want to or not, you need to talk to someone. If not me, I can call Cat and have her come over. Gretchen is covering the bar for me," he said.

Molly immediately shook her head and let him inside. The last thing she needed right now was for Cat to have any idea about what happened. Not only because it involved Shane but because Cat would ask too many questions about her powers. Powers she still had no idea how to control but at least now knew that they were tied to extreme emotional distress.

"So, what all did you see back there?" Molly asked, setting a glass of water in front of Mack.

Mack was human, and although she hadn't lost her sense of taste, she didn't keep much at home in the way of food either. She was barely home anyway with most of her time being spent at the club.

"I followed when you took off out the back door. You'd dropped your keys you were in such a hurry. After that just you seeing Shane with Carrie and having a uh... moment," he said.

"So, you saw the light?" Molly asked.

"The security light was brighter than usual for a moment if that's what you're referring to," he said before taking a sip of water.

Mack eyed Molly over his glass in a way that made her feel as if he were skirting around the issue. Like he knew exactly what she meant but was avoiding the elephant in the room. The fact that she had powers, that he'd seen her abilities and was somehow immune to the assuredly deadly force of it.

"Okay. So, what did you want to talk about?"

"It's really not my business. I'd stay out of it. I've been staying out of it but after seeing you tonight..." Mack paused and ran a frustrated hand through his hair. "Let Shane date Carrie."

"What! How do you even know her name?" Molly nearly leaped up from her chair in indignation.

"We met when I picked Shane up from rehab. Hear me out okay. For the last year, you've been all down Shane's throat about chasing after you. You wanted him to give you space, so let him give you space."

"But he came back for me! He was not supposed to fall for some pixie head tweaker!"

Mack leaned back in his chair and eyed Molly for a moment.

"He came back for himself. He made changes for himself because he needed to. Now he needs you to let him be a man without you. The obsession he had for you was unhealthy. You knew that then. You know it now. Shane's addiction wasn't to drugs, it was to you. He couldn't have you, so he turned to drugs to fill that gap. If you go back to him now, before he's redeemed himself in his eyes, that could be catastrophic. He needs to understand he can, in fact, live without you before he can live with you."

Mack was so calm, and yet Molly was furious. She stood from her chair and began to pace around the kitchen island to avoid jumping down Mack's throat. She didn't want to go too far and risk losing the one impartial person in her life at the moment.

"Do you want me to be with him or not because right now you are giving me mixed messages?"

"It's not about what I want. It's about what both of you need. What everyone needs. Just like you needed time to come into your own as a Vampire, Shane needs his time now. Not with the whole Vampire thing but with his confidence as a man. Just trust me on this. Let him date Carrie. Give him time to feel more like himself. I know that if you two are meant to be, you will come back to each other eventually. Hell, you're Vampires, you have hundreds of years if not thousands to make this work. Why rush?"

Molly stopped her pacing and leaned against the counter. Mack was right about one thing. Her feelings for Shane were too intense to be healthy. She couldn't risk her emotions getting the better of her. Especially not now when she knew it was her emotional state that triggered her powers.

"Thank you, Mack, for that bit of perspective. I'll see you tomorrow night," she said.

Mack stood and nodded before heading for the front door. Molly didn't move from her spot at the counter until she heard him pull off. When she was sure he was gone and not coming back, Molly pushed away from the counter. Her body felt heavy, and her legs felt weak, but Molly managed to make it up the stairs to her bedroom. She didn't bother changing clothes before falling face first into her mattress, too exhausted to stay awake any longer.

***

Carrie smiled as she watched Shane walking down the steps of her front porch after wishing her a good night. She had taken a risk showing up in Shane's life like she had, but there was no way she was going to give him up without a fight. She'd been enamored with him from the moment he'd walked into their group therapy session. She'd been able to see past the damage he'd done to his body through his addictions to see the brilliant and gentle man that he was. It was a shame that bitch Molly had such a hold on him. She didn't deserve him the way she trod all over his heart. Blaming him for something he'd had no control over.

Not that she knew the whole story, but Shane had been too strong of a man to succumb to addiction so easily. No only a poisonous woman could have driven such a handsome man to destruction. Especially after the atrocities he'd faced as one of Maura's Men. If Molly had broken him in a way that Maura could not, well, then she was the devil herself, and Carrie was duty bound to keep her from ever getting her claws back into Shane. No, Shane deserved much better. He deserved a better love, a true love, her love.

With Shane gone the cool breeze penetrated her thin shirt, and she went inside, making sure to lock every lock before running up to her room to daydream about Shane some more.

She just hoped that she could convince him of her love before her secret was out. Carrie had maybe a month before her father found out she was no longer in hiding and sent his goons to collect her. She hated keeping any secrets from Shane, hated that she'd been forced to lie about her supposed turning, but it was the only way for now.

Carrie picked up her new cell phone and started to dial her father's number. Maybe giving him a call would give her a little more time, but then he would know for sure she wasn't at the facility any longer. She wasn't ready to give up her hand just yet. Dealing with her father was always a game of strategy. Something she'd learned from a young age. It had taken her months to figure out just the right way to phrase things to get her father to let her go to rehab in the first place.

She'd argued its safety in anonymity and the fact that he'd be allowed to track her every move because of their therapy programs. He'd argued her exposure to unsavory Vampires and worse, humans. She'd countered with the fact that she was just as messed up. That she'd needed counseling to overcome her grief over losing her mother at such a young age. He hadn't bought that line, but she'd tried.

It wasn't until the first threat had come that he'd agreed to allow her to go. She still had no idea what the threat was, but it was enough to scare her father into letting her go if only just that little bit. It had also spurred her father to take the husband hunt a lot more seriously.

Carrie thought of the Council liaison that her father had invited to dinner shortly before the threat had come. Brody had been handsome enough and charming, but he had a slimy feel about his personality. Like beneath the polished surface there was a monster just waiting to be revealed at the most opportune moment. It also hadn't helped that her father listed all his attributes like he was reading off a menu entitled 'perfect mate material.'

Just remembering that evening made Carrie's skin crawl. No, she would wait before contacting her father. She didn't want to risk him finding her sooner than she was ready.

INDEPENDENCE

Mack stopped shelving the new liquor delivery to stare at something over Molly's shoulder. Molly might not have noticed except the rhythmic noise of bottles sliding onto the shelves was the only other noise at the moment. The club was closed, and most of the other staff wouldn't show up for another hour. Mack was only there because he acted as a liaison with the human suppliers that didn't accommodate Vampire hours. With the stunned expression on his face Molly was intrigued and a little scared. Mack wasn't the type to be surprised by anything. Hell, it had been three days, and he still hadn't mentioned a word about her seeing her powers.

Molly turned around and pressed her lips closed to keep her jaw from hitting the floor. The audacity of that woman to come here! Shane's new friend was standing at the entrance, hesitant to enter the empty cavern that the club was during nonbusiness hours. Molly stood and strode over to the woman fully aware of Mack scrambling around the bar to follow. His back up wasn't needed. She could control herself. Maybe.

"Are you lost?"

"May we help you?"

Molly and Mack said in unison. The stupid girl didn't even bother to look fazed by the tension in the room as she smiled brightly.

"Actually, I just wanted to come and introduce

myself, since I didn't get a chance to the other night. I'm Carrie."

Carrie stuck her hand out for Molly to shake. Molly stared down at the woman's hand like it was diseased and crossed her arms over her chest. This Carrie was acting as if this visit was an innocent attempt to introduce herself, but the spark of challenge was there in her gaze.

"Molly, but of course you already knew that. Well, thank you for the introduction, but I don't have time for a frivolous chat," Molly turned to walk away only to run right into Mack's chest.

She nearly fell backward from the collision. Molly hadn't realized he was so close behind her. It made her even angrier to think of how it looked to that Carrie girl. Her in Mack's arms, her lack of awareness of her surroundings. If Molly had wanted to portray that she was calm, cool, and collected about the whole situation, she failed. Molly righted herself and looked back to see Carrie already walking out the door.

"Go talk to her. If you want to know why Shane's interested. It's best if you get to know the competition," Mack said.

Molly glared and him and waved her hand in dismissal.

"That girl is no competition."

"Really, because Shane asked me about places to show her around. Date like places," Mack said with a wiggle of his eyebrow.

"I thought you wanted me to give him space to be a man," Molly said.

"Well, that was before she came here today. That was a serious power play. She wants a future with Shane, and she was putting you on notice," Mack said.

"Are you seriously mansplaining women to me right

now?"

"No, I am just stating my opinion," Mack said.

"Same difference. Get back to work, and next time, wait until I ask for back up," Molly spat at him before storming off to her office.

She hated to admit it, but Mack was right. That little brat may look cute and innocent, but Carrie was definitely a game player. The poor thing just didn't know that she was playing a losing hand. Molly may not be sure what exactly she wanted with Shane at this point, but she did know that Carrie was not the girl for him. Carrie. What kind of name was that anyway?

❈❈❈

Carrie made it about two feet from the door of Molly's club before she let the rolling laugh escape her lips. Was that woman serious? That poor woman. Molly was definitely not the imposing force she'd previously thought. Sure, she had the attitude and the body language, but it definitely wasn't backed up by her actions. If she'd wanted Carrie to believe she didn't care, Molly would have sat with her. Had a friendly chat even. Not try and fail at one-upping her power play.

As much as Carrie wanted to revel in her small victory over the woman, it still felt like a defeat. It would have been better if Molly hadn't shown that she cared about Shane. Winning him over would be a much easier battle if the love of his life wanted nothing to do with him. Still, she could work with this. Maybe if she poked at Molly enough, Carrie could coax out the devil in her. That could be fun, Carrie had always wished for a rival like the ones she'd seen in movies. Molly wasn't her tormentor, but she was a threat to her happiness with Shane.

Who knew that so much of what she had seen in

movies could be applied to actual life? Carrie hurried back to her place. She needed to finalize a few more details of her plan before she put it into action. On her way she noticed a group of teenage girls laughing and chatting together.

"Excuse me, but I'm new in town. Is there a mall nearby? I need a killer date outfit," she gushed imitating the postures and tone of voice she'd seen a million times.

The girls looked at each other before bursting out laughing and moving away. Carrie sighed, defeated. Maybe she had been a little too exaggerated with the arm movements. Thankfully, an older woman was sitting nearby and waved her over.

"The mall is about a 30-minute drive from here, my dear. If you need something sooner, there's a small boutique about a block from here. It's pricey, but they have good pieces," the woman said.

Carrie smiled and thanked the woman before following her directions to the boutique. She'd sold her car to make her escape without using her father's card. Another trick Carrie picked up from modern cinema. Technology could be scary, so many ways her father could find her once he found out she was missing. She wondered how long that would take. For all she knew, he could have found out already. He certainly had the connections and resources.

The boutique turned out to be perfect except for the prices. Carrie had gasped in shock upon seeing the numbers printed on paper slips attached to each garment. Being under her father's thumb meant all of her shopping was done for her. All she did was circle photos in a catalog or fill a cart online, and servants took care of the rest. She was suddenly regretting the cute little condo she'd rented. She was barely able to afford a simple black dress from the shop. To make matters worse, she found herself focusing on the sales person's neck, her breathing speeding up to match the rhythm of her pulse. Carrie was forced to pretend she was mute to finish the transaction and not reveal her descended canines.

Carrie needed to find blood fast, and she had no idea where. For a moment she thought about calling Shane, but that would give away her lies. As far as he knew, Carrie was a turned Vampire who'd battled her way to independence. How could she have done that without knowing how to source her own blood? She'd also told him that she'd never had blood from the source. That was a lie. They had blood servants that volunteered their services in return for a life of luxury amongst the pureblood population. She'd never tasted bagged blood until she moved to the facility. The stale swill had almost been enough to send Carrie back home.

In the movies she'd watched about Vampires, they had lured their prey with promises of sex. That wasn't something Carrie felt comfortable with. She hadn't shared her body with anyone before, and there was only one person she had ever felt the urge to share it with. Maybe Carrie could seduce Shane instead. A sip from him and she could last so much longer than on the diluted blood of any human. Carrie let her imagination run as she made her way home. Images of her naked limbs wrapped around Shane's great muscular body. His sacred parts penetrating hers in more ways than one. It should have helped, but instead, it made her hungrier.

"You look like you could use some help," a voice said from behind her.

Carrie nearly jumped out of her jeans as she whirled around on the man she hadn't realized was following her. She must have been too far into her own head to notice the other Vampire, and that wasn't good. Females were rare enough, an unattached one even scarcer. She refocused her masking efforts to make sure he couldn't sense her pureblood status. That would be disastrous.

"I'm fine, thank you," she said, hoping her voice hadn't sounded as weak and afraid to him as it did to her.

The man chuckled and shook his head.

"I could hear your stomach growling from three blocks away. A pretty thing like you, I'm surprised your sire isn't taking better care of you," he said.

"My sire is dead. I've come here for a fresh start and haven't figured out the rules of this city," she stated, unsure if she should have divulged that she was alone.

He was an unknown Vampire. Carrie had no reason to believe his intent in making contact with her was anything but seedy. Most turned Vampires kept to themselves. They didn't hold the same family structure as purebloods. They didn't have the same rules of decency. Still, it was apparent she wasn't with anyone. No way would she be walking the streets alone and so desperately hungry if she were traveling with another.

"Well, allow me to be your guide," the man reached for Carrie, but she took a step back.

The man smirked and shook his head.

"I mean you no harm, little one. This city isn't like others. We are a small population, and a starving rogue is bad for all of us. I just plan to feed you so you can be on your way," he said.

There was a hint of kindness in his eyes, but it was mixed with wariness. Carrie should have declined his offer. Gone back to her place, but her empty stomach twisted in knots at the thought of just the tiniest drop of blood. She nodded slightly and followed the man in the opposite direction of her new home. At the very least, she would learn more about the Vampires in this region and how they operated. Carrie wasn't entirely helpless. Her father had been paranoid about her safety enough to have her trained in self-defense. While Carrie had never been good at it, she knew enough to be able to escape one turned Vamp, at least.

"How far are we going?" she asked after they walked several blocks further into the downtown area.

"Not too much farther. Just to that building up ahead. If you plan to stay here, you should get acquainted with it. You will have to register yourself to receive your blood rations. They are distributed from here once a week. Of course, you could always remain rogue. In which case, you'd want to avoid this building at all costs," the Vampire said eyeing her suspiciously.

Carrie didn't need to ask why she would need to avoid the building if she were to stay rogue. She'd overheard her father cursing the rogue elements of Vampire society for as long as she could remember. Being rogue wasn't something Carrie would wish on even her worst enemy. Still, she could hardly register herself with what was bound to be a Council magistrate. They would know immediately who Carrie was. Even using the false identity that she'd used with the facility would notify her father that she was no longer under their care. The male in front of her noticed her hesitation.

"You said your sire is dead. How did that come to pass?" he asked.

"I was turned against my will. As soon as I was strong enough, I freed myself," she said, and the man nodded.

"Was there no one to exact revenge on his behalf?"

It wasn't an odd question. There were rules in place to settle differences between Vampires. A challenge or a duel was formally issued to the Council before any violent actions could take place. Of course, there were certain protections if violence occurred as self-defense. None of which applied in my made-up version of events. Turned Vampires didn't have families, but their existence relied on a series of alliances. If my fictitious sire had been part of the Vampire community, there would be allies of his that would be hunting me at this very moment.

"He was rogue. There was no one," I stated, and the man nodded.

"Well, it is still probably best if you state you knew nothing of your sire. It's uncommon but not unheard of for there to be women turned by accident. Let's get you fed before the human population floods the night streets. I wouldn't want there to be any more accidents around here," he muttered.

"Accidents?"

Carrie couldn't help but notice the shift in the man's mood when he uttered the word. The man didn't answer just led her to the building and pointed at the short line in front of a wall of windows. There were several Vampires, all men waiting and or talking to other men behind the windows. Carrie almost lost control of herself when one of the men walked away from the window carrying a small pouch that smelled of delicious blood. Even knowing that it was bagged didn't make a difference to her now. The man urged her into the line. After ten excruciating minutes, she had successfully registered as an unauthorized turn, and she had her own bag of goodies.

"Now that you are set, I must take my leave," the man said and walked away before Carrie could even thank him.

It was only then that Carrie realized she knew nothing about the man who had helped her. Not even his name. Her phone began to buzz in her pocket, and she frowned before answering it.

"I am running a little late for our appointment this evening. Something came up, but I will be there shortly. I hope you don't mind the delay," Shane's voice said, and she sighed with relief.

"It is perfectly fine. I had an errand that took longer than expected. This gives me more time to adequately prepare," Carrie replied.

"Great! I shall see you shortly," Shane said and hung up.

Carrie smiled to herself and rushed off in the direction of her house. The man who'd helped her wholly forgotten as she thought of her date with Shane. Carrie knew she still had a lot left to learn about the world, but hopefully, she wouldn't be alone in that journey much longer.

✳✳✳

Rodney slunk into the shadows as best he could to remain undetected. Two Vampires were just a few feet away from his hiding place. Their conversation was proving to be well worth the risk of being caught. As one of Maura's whelps, Rod was persona non grata amongst other Vampires. Her blood in his veins marked him for death. A death he would welcome at some point, just not right now. Not before he could free his brother from the cruel grip of their mistress.

On top of spying on the traitors, Rodney started monitoring the gossip of other Vampires as well. Being with Maura hadn't taught him a thing about Vampire society, and so it was eavesdropping on conversations like these that gave Rodney the information he needed to help plan his escape. Rod learned about the Vampire Council and pureblood Vampires. He'd also caught snippets of their sentiment and lore about Maura. To them, she was like Jack the Ripper and Freddie Cougar rolled into one. Maura was the monster lurking in the shadows to destroy them at any moment. Rodney couldn't help but agree with their summation.

Maura was, in fact, a monster. She was lurking in the shadows waiting for the most opportune time to strike. These men, however, weren't her target. These men were nothing to her. Lowly turned Vampires good for nothing but the gossip they spread. Turned Vampires, Rodney had learned, were solitary in nature, but with the return of Maura, even they had begun to close their ranks. Gearing up for when the boogeyman made her appearance.

"I'm telling you, this girl was pureblood. She tried to hide it, but in her hunger, she let her walls slip," one of the men said.

"You sure they didn't slip something in your drink at the bar?" the other man chuckled.

"If she sticks around, you'll see for yourself," the man said.

"Look ain't no pureblood female running around unattended. You sure you didn't just run into one of the tainted women? Maybe she fell to one of Maura's Men like them others and then changed her mind once she saw the evil in him," the man said.

"I know a pureblood when I see one. The girl wasn't tainted like the others," the first man said.

"I'm older than you, so I'll be the judge of that," The second man said before stalking off down the street.

Rodney let out the breath he hadn't realized he was holding. It was unlikely that either man had ever come across a pureblood. Still, if this new woman was as different as they said, it stood to reason she was connected to the traitors in some way. Rodney kept his distance as he followed the men around town.

"There she is! I told you," the first man said stopping across the street from the town theater.

A small, blonde woman stood at the entrance, a tiny black dress doing its best to make her slight body look enticing. She was too slim for Rodney's tastes. He preferred a woman with more bounty in their bosom and backside. Not that any woman really gave him a second look. He wasn't a handsome man, and his father's right hook had left his nose deformed in such a way that his voice had never matured to a manly depth as his brother's had.

Rod should have let Axel take some of the beatings from that bastard. Then maybe Rod's growth wouldn't have been so stunted from countless injuries left untended. It was a miracle Rod was able to walk given how many times the old man had broken his legs.

"And I was right, too. Look who she's meeting. Next time don't waste your time. She's just as tainted as them others. If you're really that hard up, maybe you could petition for a turning permit. You're of age now," The other man said breaking Rod out of his self-pity party.

He turned his gaze back to where the woman stood in time to see the Grim Reaper embrace the tiny woman. He shook his head. The man wasn't a walking corpse any longer. His was still tall and slim but his chest was broader and his arms bulged with muscle against the shirt he wore. This wasn't good. If the man had regained his health, he would be harder to dispatch when the time came. Maura was not going to like this development. As far as the girl, he would keep that bit of news to himself for now. At least until he was able to learn more about her.

❋❋❋

Molly pulled her coat tighter around her body as the chilly night breeze swept the crowded streets. Despite the chill in the air people were still out and about enjoying the last few nights suitable enough for outdoor activities.

"Just like old times. You and me out for a girl's night," Cat said with a mischievous smile.

"Sure, but why tonight? Why not give me a heads up so maybe I could have gotten a replacement for Gretchen?" Molly asked.

"Gretchen doesn't mind. She isn't big on psychological thrillers," Cat replied.

Molly snorted and rolled her eyes.

"Neither am I. I much prefer romances, and you know that," she said.

"True, but I didn't want to go alone. With Xander on Maura patrol, it's rare that he finds time to indulge my old human habits," Cat said.

"Shane loves psychological thrillers, why not ask him? I know he isn't exactly on patrol lately. This would be the perfect outing to take his mind off the fact that the others still aren't convinced he's ready to fight," Molly said.

Cat glared at Molly.

"Can't we just hang out? I'm trying to have fun here and not think about Maura or the fact that we're constantly on watch," Cat snapped.

Molly stopped and pulled her friend into a hug.

"I'm sorry, Cat. I know this has been rough on you too. I at least have my club to keep me preoccupied," Molly said.

Cat relaxed into her embrace. Molly was just about to let go when she heard Cat's muffled sniffling.

"Are you crying?"

"No," Cat muttered, but her voice was thick.

"Okay. I'll give you three minutes to not cry on my shoulder, but any longer and we are going to be late for the movie," Molly said.

Cat chuckled a little and clung tighter to her. Molly rubbed Cat's back, comforting her best friend as best she could in the middle of the crowded sidewalk. With everything that had been going on in her life, Molly should have known that this spur of the moment outing wasn't just about sisterly bonding. Cat was dealing with just as much, only she didn't have anything to distract her. Sure, she had her consulting business, but that was mostly a solitary thing. The Shadow wasn't a friendly visitor as far as Molly was concerned. Gretchen was either with Claude or working at the club. Xander had been patrolling more frequently. Shane had only just returned from rehab, but apparently, that Carrie girl was occupying his time.

As if thoughts could conjure, Molly glanced across the street and saw Shane and Carrie sharing gelato at the Italian café. It had been one of the places Molly had marked for a future date with Shane, at least before the accident. Obviously, they'd never made it, and now here he was with that girl. They looked cute together. Carrie's light to Shane's dark, her cheerleader to his suave professor. It was enough to turn Molly's stomach.

"Ouch!"

Cat pulled out of Molly's grasp and glared at her.

"Sorry, I got lost in my head. I didn't realize," Molly rambled but never took her eyes off Carrie and Shane.

Cat shook her head.

"It's fine, just let me know next time you feel your powers getting out of hand," she said.

"Yeah, sorry. Why don't you go ahead to the theater and get seats? I need a moment to get myself together," Molly said.

"No problem. Just don't take too long and make sure you get popcorn," Cat said.

"Of course, extra buttery," Molly smiled and forced her gaze to her best friend and away from Shane and Carrie.

Cat smiled back and patted Molly's arm gently before walking down the street. Molly waited until she knew Cat wasn't going to turn back before she took a deep breath and headed straight for Shane and Carrie. It was a bad idea, especially with her powers apparently out of control again. Still, Molly made her way over and pasted a big smile on her face. She wanted to make her presence known, but that didn't mean she wanted either of them to know how upset she was.

Carrie saw Molly first and slid her hand into Shane's which had been resting casually on the table. A blatant possessive move. Shane glanced briefly at her hand in his before closing his around it. At least until he followed Carrie's gaze and saw Molly standing there.

"Molly," Shane said sliding his hand to his lap and away from Carrie.

His face flushed red as if embarrassed to be seen with Carrie. That bolstered Molly's courage at the same time that it crushed her heart. Sure, he was being considerate by not flaunting his new relationship, but it apparently was a relationship. Otherwise, he wouldn't be so guilty.

"Shane," Molly bit out.

There was an awkward pause before Carrie spoke.

"It's nice seeing you again, Molly. Would you care to join us?" Carrie asked.

Molly shot a glare in the woman's directions. Hell no, she didn't want to join them. What she wanted was to drag the tiny woman into an alley and show her just what she was up against.

"Again? I wasn't aware you two had met," Shane said.

"Carrie came by my club to introduce herself. I'm surprised she didn't mention it. You apparently gave her the wrong idea about our relationship status," Molly said with a raised eyebrow.

Shane squirmed in his chair. He was nervous, and that made Molly happy. He should be uncomfortable.

"Wrong idea?"

"Young Carrie here thought that we were somehow more than friends. You must have neglected to tell her why we broke up. Did you not want to tarnish her high opinion of you?" Molly asked.

"Molly," Shane said sounding defeated.

"I don't care about the past. I know who Shane is now, and that's all that matters," Carrie said brightly.

Shane seemed to relax a little, and that wasn't what Molly wanted. This girl was delusional, and that was fine. Molly didn't care about Carrie. Molly cared about Shane. If Carrie was his choice, she needed to know the truth. She needed to know what Shane was capable of. The reason that all it would take was a word from Molly to have Shane crawling back into her arms.

"I thought that once too. Then Shane left me headless on the side of a road," Molly made a show of checking her watch, "You two enjoy your evening."

Molly turned and marched away from the couple. Shane and Carrie both sat in stunned silence as she left. Molly should have felt better, she should have felt relief. Instead, she still just felt sick and heartbroken. Shane was moving on from her. Maybe it was time she did the same. Without thinking about it, Molly pulled out her phone and dialed Brody's number. It rung twice before she cursed and hung up. Brody was the last man she should be calling. No matter what happened with Shane, Brody was not the solution.

"You forgot the popcorn," Cat hissed as Molly joined

her in the theater.

Molly rolled her eyes and dropped her coat in the empty seat next to her best friend.

"I'll be back," Molly muttered and headed back to the concession stand.

Apparently, it had been long enough for Cat to get over her moment of weakness. At least one of them would be having a good night. After the movie Cat would surely head back to her loving mate while Molly went home alone. She was tired of being alone, but maybe that was for the best. Her taste in men wasn't the greatest. Before Shane, her human boyfriend had been controlling and possessive. Shane proved less than dedicated, and Brody who was more interested in her body than her brain. Yeah, maybe Molly needed to stay focused on herself awhile longer.

CARNIVAL

Brody could barely contain his anger as he saw Carolina smiling lovingly at that abomination. Outside of a human carnival at that. He had to chalk it up to the excessive force of Maura's demon blood running through the man's body. There was no way a woman of such high standing could possibly fall for such a monster. Brody did his best not to acknowledge the sting of rejection in his chest. A second woman meant to be his was now in the thrall of that thing.

Granted the man was much better looking now than he had been when Brody had met him months ago. He had to have fallen back into favor with Maura. That was the only magic that could bring a man back from the edge of death so quickly. That or the life force of a pureblood. Brody snarled thinking of the possibility that Carolina had given herself entirely to the other man.

Carolina had been promised to him. She was his to take and reap the benefits of her sweet bounty. He'd kissed her father's ass long enough to deserve the honor. How dare she ruin her purity before he could acquire it! Brody fought the urge to get out of the car. When Maximus requested his help in finding his daughter, the last place Brody expected to discover her was here with that thing.

With Maura on the loose, Vampires in the area

had been circling their wagons so to speak. Either by picking up and moving to less treacherous pastures or feeding news and gossip to the authorities to aid in her capture. That is how he'd come across the rumors of an unattached pureblood female in town. He hadn't wanted to believe the story, but the poor man had described Carolina precisely as he remembered her. A small pixie of a woman with an air of mischief that left one unsure if she were a Vampire or something else entirely. She exuded confidence that only came from years of people catering to your every whim.

Brody had been anxious to get her into his bed after their first encounter. Not just because of the connections and status he would gain because of it. No, Carolina, like Molly, needed a firm hand to break that insolent streak they both possessed. Alas, this situation would prove to be advantageous in other ways. If Maximus knew his daughter was being courted by one of Maura's Men, he would destroy them all with no question. With that deviant out of the way, Brody would have a clear field to conquer both women with little retribution.

Molly was already a scorned woman. She would be in desperate need of his influence and lonely enough to be brought to her knees before him. Molly had called him out of the blue. She was already regretting her decision to reject him and would be easy to conquer once this situation played itself out. Carolina was now a ruined woman. No one would want her now that she was tainted. Maximus would probably rush their mating to cover the grievous affront to his bloodline. That would leave Brody to do as he pleased with her. That thought alone is what kept Brody from storming across the street and making his presence known. Instead, he pulled his phone from his pocket and dialed Maximus' private line.

"You better not have disturbed me with more bad news," Maximus snapped.

Brody resisted the urge to just hang up at the man's ill-mannered response.

"I've found, Carolina. I cannot extract her as of yet, but I have news that's best delivered in person," Brody was purposely vague in his wording.

He wanted to make the man squirm a bit before giving him the assurances he needed. Maximus was powerful and entitled. Brody had once looked up to the man, at least until he'd gotten to know him. Maximus was just as power-mad and vengeful as the very creature he'd vowed to destroy. It wasn't just a rumor about his ancestor being the one who had sired Maura. It was his bloodline that was responsible for the horrors she had committed. Still, the man was intent on recreating the conditions that had brought Maura into her power. Maximus had several magic slaves in his possession. The keeping of slaves was frowned upon in Vampire society. Not to say that other means of demeaning servitude weren't employed, but actual slaves were no longer the norm. Maximus only got away with his madness by claiming the women in his care were willing participants. He had enough sway in the world that no one dared question it.

"You will bring my daughter to me at once," Maximus demanded.

"If that were possible I would. Like I said there are things I must discuss with you in person. I will be at your doorstep by tomorrow," Brody hung up before the man could threaten him any longer.

Brody got in his vehicle and drove off. His headlights lighting up the alley across from where he parked. A thin weasel-like man stood in the alley's darkness staring directly at him. A moment of recognition hit

Brody. He'd seen the man a few times when visiting Molly at her club. Something had never felt right about the man, but Brody chalked it up to his less than pleasant face. He was likely a rogue spy, keeping tabs on regular Vampire society for his rogue master.

Under normal circumstances, Brody would have stopped to take care of the man. Most rogues held loose loyalty and could easily be paid to keep quiet about things of importance they may have overheard. However, tonight he didn't have the patience nor the time. He had to get to Maximus quickly before he lost his small window of opportunity to manipulate the outcome of this story.

❀❀❀

"Care to finally tell me what brings you to the area?" Shane asked.

Shane waited with Carrie in line for the next attraction at the local carnival. This whole date was a bad idea, but he'd promised Mack and Cat that he would at least make an effort to see if Carrie could be more than just a friend. After the awkward evening with Molly, he couldn't say their concerns were unwarranted.

Carrie was a sweet enough girl. They had pleasant conversations, and she was already a Vampire, one who didn't mind he was one of Maura's Men. He hated that moniker, but unfortunately, that was how he and the others were known to the Vampire world.

Normally, Shane wouldn't be caught dead anywhere near a place like this. It held too many memories of happier times. It was at this same carnival so many years ago that he'd finally confessed to Molly that he was a Vampire. He'd wholly expected her to think him insane. Or worse yet fawn all over him like some Vampire crazed teenager, but she had surprised him.

She'd asked thoughtful questions and been the perfect amount of distrustful and understanding.

It had also been the first and only time since his escape from Maura that he'd taken human blood from the source. He could remember the way her pulse jumped. How her scent had changed from anxious to aroused when his canines pierced the tender flesh of her neck. He hadn't taken much just a small taste, but it had been enough to have him embarrassing himself like a prepubescent boy. Especially when another part of his anatomy had pierced an even more sacred flesh.

"Shane," Carrie's voice brought him back to reality.

Shane shifted uncomfortably with the clear bulge in his pants. His arousal hadn't escaped Carrie's notice. She smirked before slipping her hand into his.

"We're next," she said.

Shane forced a smile onto his face as he handed their tickets to the acne-riddled teen manning the ride.

"I'm sorry I zoned out earlier, but can you tell me again? What brought you to my neck of the woods?" he asked once they had passed the attraction gates.

Carrie smiled before leaning over to place a kiss on his lips. Shane was shocked into silence. He had been only slightly aware that her friendship had somehow crossed into a mild infatuation, but he had been very clear about where his heart resided.

"I know you are in love with someone else, but I firmly believe there is something between us that begs to be explored," she said before pulling the safety bar down to their laps. Locking him in the now uncomfortably small car.

Before he could escape the cars began to move, and he realized with dismay that they were on one of the longest rides at the event. Dubiously named the Love Canal.

✼✼✼

Carrie knew almost as soon as she'd kissed him that she'd moved too quickly. If her father credited her with anything, it was her stubbornness. It still hurt knowing that he had become so aroused by the thought of another woman in her presence. It didn't matter that Shane's heart was still with someone else. She hadn't been able to help herself. He was smart, funny, and gorgeous. He checked all the boxes on every woman's must-have list, and here he was wasting away because of one woman's refusal to forgive.

No, she wouldn't sit idly by and pine for him. That just wasn't her style, and well frankly, the man needed to know he had options. That Molly must have no idea what she'd cast aside. If Shane were to try to move on, Carrie was glad to help him with that. Still, she had to come up with something to ease the tense mood. It would do her no good if Shane took off as soon as the ride was over. She had to salvage their friendship at least if she hoped to have any chance of getting him to recognize their relationship as something more.

"Carrie. I cannot lie to you and say that my heart will be swayed," Shane began, but Carrie put her hand over his mouth.

"Don't say it. Don't push me away because my feelings for you are more than you expected," Carrie said, hating the vulnerability in her voice.

"You are a sweet girl, but I don't care about you in that way," he said with a finality that almost crushed her.

"Like I said. I know you are in love with someone else, but my feelings won't allow me to just give up without trying. Please just allow me the pursuit even if I fail. It will be better than not trying at all. Give me an honest shot. Give yourself a chance at happiness without all the drama," she urged, and a small smile touched his lips.

A sign that gave her hope that maybe he just might have some interest in her after all.

"I'm sorry. I hope you will still come to the dinner tomorrow evening. The party is just as much a celebration for you as it is for me. I wouldn't have come this far as fast without your continued friendship," Shane said.

"I will be there as your friend, but my affections won't be easily dismissed," Carrie stated.

They rounded the bend back to the start, and it seemed Shane couldn't get out of the ride car fast enough.

"You are an amazing woman, Carrie. You deserve more than I could ever offer you," Shane said.

He placed a chaste kiss on her cheek and walked away. Carrie stood there at the exit of the ride, frustrated and alone. She would still go to the dinner at his home. If she had any chance of changing his mind it meant she needed back up and what better back up to have than the endorsement of those closest to him.

❀❀❀

When Shane left Carrie at the carnival, he hadn't had a destination in mind. He hadn't wanted to go back to the mansion, where Cat would undoubtedly question him about his date with Carrie. It hadn't been a date. At least not for him. His heart was with Molly. Even if he wanted to move on, Shane didn't think he could.

Being at the carnival had brought back too many memories. It had been a bad idea to begin with. Shane kept walking, trying to clear his head, trying to come up with a plan of action. Shane needed to win his woman back. He'd decided to give her space. Shane tried to see

Carrie as someone he could be with, but there was no substitute for true love. He deserved a happy ending with Molly.

"What are you doing here?"

Molly opened her front door just enough to peak her head out. It was late, the sun was rising, and he knew she was tired from a long night at the Club Obelisk. Still, he'd had come to see her. Had to make his feelings clear one more time.

"I want to talk," he said lamely.

His confidence failing under her withering glare.

"Shouldn't you be snuggling with your new girlfriend at this hour?"

"Carrie is not my girlfriend. Can I come inside? I didn't think I would be out this late, and I don't have my shielded glasses," he said.

Molly looked as if she were going to slam the door in his face, but thankfully she opened the door enough for him to slip inside. As soon as he was across the threshold, he pulled her into his arms.

"I thought you wanted to talk," she said.

Her tone full of attitude but the softness of her body in his arms belied her true feelings.

"Talking can wait. There is something I want to do first."

Shane bent down and brushed his lips across hers. Just the barest whisper of soft skin on skin yet heat shot between them as if he'd devoured her.

"Shane," she gasped.

It was a plea for more. A request Shane would never deny. His mouth crushed to hers, letting the emotion run freely between them. Molly's hands encircled him, running along his back and sides. Her nails raking over his clothing. She was hot and delicious, but as much as Shane wished to indulge the need to take her, he knew that he needed to talk to her first. He needed to make it clear what was in his heart.

"Molly, please. We need to talk," Shane said.

He took a step back, putting enough room between them to cool the raging fires of lust.

"Fine," Molly breathed and gestured for him to follow her further into her home.

She made them both a cup of blood before sitting across from him at the small kitchen table.

"We haven't had a chance to really talk since I came back from rehab," Shane began.

"Maybe because you've been too busy with that girl," Molly snorted over her steaming cup.

"She is my friend. She helped me a lot during my therapy. It would be rude of me to ignore her during her stay," Shane said.

"Yet ignoring me is perfectly fine."

This talk was not going how he expected. Granted he hadn't even been sure Molly would open the door for him. During therapy, he'd been able to talk to Cat a few times. She'd mentioned how much everyone missed him, including Molly. Yet when he'd shown up, she acted as if he wasn't there. He'd been all but invisible to her unless it was to shoot barbs about his relationship with Carrie. Shane was tired of her venomous attitude.

"You've been the one ignoring me!"

Molly looked stricken. Shane had never raised his voice at her, but he couldn't hold back his anger at that moment, any more than he could hold back his love for her any other time.

"I'm sorry. This isn't what I wanted. I love you, Molly. I have always loved you. I don't know if there is anything more I could possibly do to prove that to you. I mean, I've gotten my shit together, I gave you the space you said you needed. I am here before you now to profess my love," Shane said.

Molly's gaze softened. She set her mug down.

"Your love was never in question. It was your commitment to that love. I'm not the same girl I was before. Pretty words no longer sway me. It's your actions I take issue with. You claim you have made all of this change for me, but you haven't shown it to be true. Honestly, you shouldn't have changed for me. You should have changed for you."

Shane hated how much Molly sounded like Dr. Hartford. He'd been released from rehab because of his progress, but Dr. Hartford had warned that his journey to recovery was only just beginning. That he had lots more road to travel before he was ready to be intimate with anyone again.

✾✾✾

Molly sat waiting for Shane to speak. She hadn't expected him to visit at that hour, but she was glad he had. He'd been right. They did need to talk. There was a lot to talk about, but Molly really just wanted to get back to the steamy kisses of before. It had been so long since they'd shared that heat, that intensity. She wanted more, and she was almost willing to forget everything to have it. She would have if Shane didn't push her away.

So, there they sat in Molly's kitchen over a mug of blood. The heat of passion between them quickly cooling to the simmering anger of before. Molly may have been able to see things from his perspective, but Shane was refusing to see them from hers. He still thought that all he had to do was show up on his terms and profess his love. It would take much more than that. Especially now with that Carrie girl in the picture.

"I know I have a lot to work on. I'm just asking

131

that you give us a chance. Tonight when I was at the carnival with Carrie, she kissed me, and I knew I'd made a mistake. That she could never replace you," Shane finally spoke.

Molly saw red as soon as Shane mentioned his date. He'd taken Carrie there of all places. She'd been able to forgive him for everything else, but the carnival was their place. The place where he'd confessed himself to her before taking her body and her blood. That place was sacred, that memory was now tarnished in her mind.

"Get out."

Molly was too angry to yell. Too heartbroken to do much more than sit there and grip her mug to keep from reaching across the table and strangling him.

"Molly," he said softly, but she shook her head.

Her skin already tingling with the powerful light of destruction within her. She knew Shane saw it there, glowing just beneath the surface. Could feel the prickling heat along his skin just as she did. He stood and headed to the door.

"We'll talk again later. After dinner tomorrow, okay," Shane said.

She held on as long as she could. Long after she heard the door close and Shane's footsteps retreating from her property. She held on until the world began to fade around her, and she prayed. She prayed she wouldn't destroy everything she owned as the light encompassed her.

DINNER PARTY

Maura prowled the warehouse looking over her army as they trained. The time had come, and yet her army was only at half the strength she required. No matter, taking her revenge on the three males that had escaped her was only the first item on her grand agenda. What better way to start her quest for world domination than to rid the world of those who had crossed her in the past. Xander, Claude, and Shane would die first. Then Maura would drain that nuisance of a girl, Molly, for everything she was worth. Not that it would be much, but Maura's full power would be restored to her, and nothing could stop her once that happened.

"My Queen," A trainee bowed as she passed.

Maura didn't spare him a glance. There were too many, and they were far too expendable to warrant Maura wasting her time to get to know them. All that mattered was they give her the proper respect and do anything she asked exactly how she asked them to do it. Only a select few had earned any extra attention. It was those few who awaited her now. It had been a week since she was last updated on the progress of her army. They better have good news for her today.

She made her way to the office loft and glared down at her minions who kneeled before her. "Speak!"

"The new weapons sh-sh-shipment arrived Tuesday.

I've gone over each p-p-piece my-myself. Everyth-th-th-thing is as it should be. No mistakes th-th-this time," Henry barely made it through his report.

Maura wasn't sure if he was defective or just scared of her. He had every right to be scared considering his predecessor had bled out at his feet just last week when said mistake was reported. His stuttering was annoying. If Henry didn't correct it, he would be replaced as well. She'd only allowed him the privilege of being known at Rodney's insistence that he was the best candidate.

She waved her hand for the next person to start.

"The steroid mixture has caused some men to be hyper-aggressive, almost animalistic. They have been separated from the population to help maintain our numbers," Axel reported a smug grin on his face.

Maura glared back at him. He may be her current favorite, at least in the bedroom, but that didn't mean he was any higher in supposed rank than anyone else. He was getting too cocky. Maura would enjoy bringing him down a few pegs later on that night. She squeezed her thighs together as moisture pooled between them. The thought of Axel strapped to her bed of needles, blood pouring from wounds reopened by her barbed whip. It was almost too much for her to keep her composure and continue with the reports. Nevertheless, the progression of her plan was more important than a little fun. With another wave of her hands, it was Rodney's turn.

"All the accounts are in order. The traitors are all holed away in their mansion, although they frequent Molly's establishment. I have also heard the news that a Council member will be coming soon. Apparently one of them has an estranged daughter who happens to be in town."

Maura hated Rodney the weasel more than any of

her other men, maybe even more than the traitors, but he had proved himself valuable many times over. One of those times being now.

"A daughter you say?"

"Yes, and it seems she has taken a fancy to one of the traitors," Rodney confirmed.

"I want her. Bring her to me immediately," Maura said and strode from the room.

She would be having a very special guest soon and needed to be well prepared. A daughter of the Council, a pureblood would soon be in her grasp. It was only made sweeter that she had connections to the traitors. No need to ferret out her prey when this one key player would bring them all running her way.

❋❋❋

Cat watched in amusement as jealousy crossed her best friend's face. After the past year, there was no way of knowing how Molly would react to seeing Shane with someone else. It had been a gamble for sure inviting a new friend to dinner with Molly there, but at least it was proving entertaining. Cat of course had hoped it would finally push her friend passed her stubborn resolve to hate Shane when they were meant to be together.

"You shouldn't push her like this," Gretchen said in a hushed tone.

Cat smirked.

"She needs it. Quite frankly I'm tired of hearing her bitch," she didn't lower her voice.

Molly shot her a glare, and Cat returned one in kind. Claude chuckled from across the room, and Molly's eyes literally sparked with anger. Her pupils slowly fading away as a bright light emanated from them. Everyone in the room froze. It was getting more frequent that signs of Molly's mysterious powers were showing. Considering the last time it was unleashed she had somehow bested Maura, it scared the shit out of pretty much everyone.

Gretchen, who had unofficially become the peacemaker of the group, whispered something in Molly's ear, and the eerie, white light dissipated. With all the attention now on her, Molly got up and left without so much as a goodbye. Shane whispered something to Carrie and took off after Molly.

"Was that really necessary?" Xander asked pulling Cat into his arms before she could follow Molly out.

"She needs to let it go, and the more we baby her, the worse it will be. I will not see this family torn apart because of her unwillingness to forgive," she said.

"You need to drop this, whatever it is you have planned," he said.

"Not happening," she replied

"Have you ever thought that maybe if you weren't always meddling that things would work out for themselves?" he asked.

She shook her head.

"Tell that to your ex-girlfriend," Cat huffed, touching the heavy chain around her neck.

The necklace stuck on Cat's neck a reminder of Xander's past and the key to Maura's powers. Xander growled before kissing her soundly and storming out of the room. A habit he had any time he was reminded of the perils she'd gone through at the start of their relationship.

"Thank you for inviting me to your home. I'm sorry if I caused any awkwardness for your friend," Carrie said suddenly and ran from the room.

Cat felt sorry for the girl. For the first time, Cat realized that Molly and Shane weren't the only people whose feelings were involved here. Greg followed

Carrie, and Claude pulled Gretchen from the room before she could say anything to Cat. It didn't matter. Cat knew she'd been the one in the wrong here. She didn't need her friend's lecture. Tonight should have been about celebrating Shane's recovery. That was the reason they had all gathered there. Instead, Cat allowed the Shadow's demands to supersede her judgment. The party had been a disaster from the start.

✿✿✿

Shane had no idea what had Molly so riled up, but he knew he couldn't just let her leave the party so upset. He apologized to Carrie and stood to follow.

"Good Luck," Carrie said softly, disappointment in her eyes.

Carrie would always just be a friend to Shane. Molly was, and always would be, the woman for him. He could no longer demure to others' feelings. Play these silly games of will they or won't they.

"Thank you," he said and rushed from the room.

Molly wasn't in the hall, and by the time he made it to the door, she was sliding into her red sports car. Without thinking, he got into the passenger seat. She turned to face him, her eyes shooting daggers at him, but he didn't care.

"Get out," she snapped.

Shane reached over and pulled her into his arms. He fully expected a struggle. Shane was relieved when she sank into his embrace. Molly may be mad at him, but her body knew him as a source of comfort.

"Why are you here?" she asked after a moment.

"You know why I'm here," Shane sighed.

Molly pulled away from him. She didn't look him in the eye. At this point, he was used to it. She hated him, was disgusted by him. Still, he loved her with all of his

137

heart. One horrific twist of fate had ruined everything between them. If Shane could take it back, he would. If had learned anything in his life it was that dwelling on the past was a dangerous thing. Molly hadn't been the only one affected by the tragedy. She just refused to see it.

"I'm sure your girlfriend doesn't appreciate you chasing after me," she spat.

Shane couldn't help the smile that crept onto his face. Molly was jealous. She kept her face turned away from him, but he could see her reflection in the window. Her lips were pursed almost in a pout as she spoke. It made his heart swell. Gave him hope.

❈❈❈

Molly couldn't look at Shane. There was too much emotion coursing through her to remain aloof. She wasn't jealous, at least not entirely. No, she was pissed. How dare he claim he would never let her go! Then, after a month away, come back looking like the man she had once loved but now on the arm of another. Of course, she should be over it by now. It had been a month since she'd first seen them together. A week since she crashed their date and spilled the beans about his betrayal. Only for the woman to shrug it off and continue to stare longingly at Shane.

"Carrie? She's just a friend, she means nothing compared to you," he said.

Molly tensed at Shane's words. She never wanted to hear that name again. It tore at her heart to know that he could possibly feel for someone else the way he claimed to feel about her.

"Save your platitudes for someone who cares and get out," she said.

There was no venom in her voice. Shane had hurt

138

her more than anyone in her entire life. That was really saying something considering what she'd gone through as a red headed, foster child. Molly had trusted him with her life. He'd failed her. Molly had died, and he'd left her to her fate. She trusted him with her heart, and now Shane was shoving it back in her face.

"I'm not leaving. Not this time. You can push and scream, do whatever you want, but I'm not leaving you ever again," he said.

One glance in his direction was enough for Molly to know he meant it. Not that she had needed to, the conviction was there in his voice. Every alarm bell in her head was screaming for her to run far, far away. Her stubborn, stupid heart had other ideas where Shane was concerned. No matter how much Molly denied it, she still loved him. She knew it, and he did too. Not sure of what else to do, Molly turned on her car and drove off. She didn't want to be anywhere near the mansion at the moment. Didn't want anyone else to see her like this.

"You want me to trust you, but you make it so hard," Molly said when she pulled into her garage.

Shane climbed out of her car and walked around to open her door. She got out and let him pull her into his arms.

"Then don't trust me. Trust your heart," Shane said brushing a finger across Molly's collarbone.

Her breath hitched. Molly closed her eyes. Letting the heat of his gaze and warmth of his body envelope her.

"What if my heart says it wants you to go home," she asked.

Her eyes fluttered open but avoided his. She knew he could tell she was lying. Her heart was saying the exact opposite.

"My home is wherever you are," he said.

Of course, he couldn't make this easy for her. Molly stood on tiptoe and kissed him. Shane groaned, accepting her surrender. His grip tightened around her waist, and Molly found herself being hoisted off the ground. Shane cradled her in his arms.

"What are you doing?" she breathed between kisses.

"Isn't it customary for the man to carry his woman across the threshold?" he asked with a smirk.

"That's a man and wife entering their new home for the first time," Molly clarified.

"Exactly," Shane said.

He crushed his mouth to hers, stifling any protest she could have made. Shane carried Molly into the house and up to her bedroom. She tore at their clothes as they made their way up. Vampire strength came in handy for pesky clothes when all she wanted was to feel his bare skin against hers.

"Once I have you know there is no turning back. You are mine and mine only, do you understand?" Shane asked.

He stood above her at the edge of the bed, tall and proud. Naked as the day he was born, and god was the man glorious and erect before her.

"You stubborn bastard," she cursed under her breath, but to be honest, his new take-charge attitude was a major turn on.

"Stubborn and madly in love," Shane replied.

Molly could fight all she wanted. It didn't mean she wasn't still attracted to Shane. Even when he'd been an emaciated drug addicted skeleton, she'd been enticed by the memory of him. Maybe it was lingering affection or nostalgia for what once was between them, but tonight, Molly decided when she saw him lounging on her bed. Tonight, she would have him. Take what he offered, what her heart demanded and tomorrow, well, tomorrow she'd figure out her next move.

❅❅❅

He fought the urge to rub his chest where her words had hit like an arrow to the heart. She was skeptical of his love, skeptical of him. Still, this was progress. Molly didn't outright deny him. If she had insisted that he leave, he would have. Thankfully, she hadn't. Molly played along, allowing him to stay and now? Now was the big time. It was now or never. She either accepted him and everything he had to offer, or he would be forced to tuck his tail and run home a sad, heartbroken puppy once again.

"Show me," Molly moaned gripping her breasts and fondling them in full view.

Shane's dick twitched with arousal. How he'd missed this, seeing her playful and wanton in bed. Playing with herself, priming her body for him. Shane surged forward replacing her fingers with his tongue.

"Like this?" he laved at her flesh. Softly, tentatively at first before latching on completely, suckling her with just enough force to extend her nipples before rolling them with his tongue.

"Yes," Molly gasped and gripped his shoulders.

He glanced up to see her head thrown back, her pink lip caught beneath her teeth. She was holding back, and that was the last thing he wanted. He continued his oral onslaught, catching her nipple with his teeth for a playful nip all the while his hand slid down her body and found the neat pile of soft curls between her legs. Shane still didn't quite understand the modern woman's obsession with looking like a prepubescent and was glad that Molly hadn't followed the trend in that regard.

141

"Open for me," he commanded.

Molly whimpered before widening her legs, his body sliding fully between them. He repositioned himself to keep his full weight from crushing her. Molly sat up and captured his mouth. Her warm tongue sliding along his and almost making him forget all about foreplay. He indulged her for a moment before taking her breath away as he slipped at first one finger inside. Testing the waters so to speak.

"More," she sang into his mouth.

It was the sweet song of a woman in heat. His woman in heat. Shane continued to stroke her with his finger until it was sufficiently slick with her arousal. He pulled his hand away from her and brought it to his mouth. She watched him intently, fire in her eyes, as he tasted her juices.

"Mmmm, I'll definitely be having more of that later."

"Later?" Molly quipped, "Why not now?"

"Because this is just the appetizer, and I fully intend to finish the entire five-course meal before getting to dessert," Shane said.

"Five courses?" She asked.

"Five courses and I intend to enjoy every, last, bite."

He punctuated the last few words with soft kisses from her shoulder to her neck, allowing his canines to graze the sensitive skin above her jugular. He felt her tense slightly. Shane backed away, trailing kisses back down before lingering at her collarbone.

"But only if you allow," Shane clarified.

He paused looking into her eyes, waiting, praying that he hadn't just screwed up big time.

"Let's cross that bridge when we get there," she finally said.

Relieved Shane laughed and kissed her delving his finger back inside. Doing his best to restore the hot and bothered mood of before. Her body softened, relaxing underneath him, and he took this moment before she changed her mind, sliding a second finger into her depths. Twisting and swirling along her slick inner walls until he found the precise spot he was looking for. Shane smiled down at Molly as her face contorted in orgasmic bliss, her inner muscles pulsating around his fingers.

"Oh my god, yes!"

Molly may have changed because of what happened, but this one thing he was overjoyed to know was the same. She'd always been a very responsive lover. It drove Shane wild with the desire to see, hear, and feel all the ways she expressed her sexual desires. Shane pressed his thumb firmly against her clit as he slid his fingers from her. Tracing slow circles as he shifted down to position his mouth at her core. Usually, he'd play with her a bit more. Explore her body with his hands and tease her until she was begging for release. This time, he was the impatient one.

"I thought you planned to enjoy the full five courses," she gasped as his tongue flicked playfully over her already sensitive bud.

"I do, but there's nothing wrong with skipping to dessert a little early," Shane said.

He'd wasted too much time away from her to take his time now. He dove right in devouring her, drowning himself in her arousal. His canines extended as her rapid heart rate increased the throbbing of a nearby artery. He pulled back a little, just enough to look her in the eye. A silent plea for her permission to taste all of her in his eyes. He waited until she gave a slight nod of her head before he struck, sinking his teeth into her flesh.

Molly bucked against him crying out in pleasure as

her climax and blood filled his mouth. He took her into him. The primal beast inside roared in triumph as he slid up her body and seated his manhood within her. Molly's legs wrapped tightly around his hips locking him into position above her, her hands dug into the sheets twisting them tightly in her grasp as she frantically rocked her hips against him.

"Mine," Shane heard himself growl as if it were truly a beast inside him and not his own voice.

Beads of sweat dripped down Shane's body as he tried to maintain control. As he fought his own release to ensure he made good on his promise to always thoroughly pleasure her before his own release, but his effort was futile. His hips matched hers. Thrust for thrust. The only sensation he could discern over the roar of his impending orgasm was the rhythmic slapping of their bodies and Molly's unrestrained screams of pleasure. Like a ticking time bomb, tick, tick, tick, boom. He exploded, his hips locking with hers like the horns of two fighting bulls before he collapsed on top of her thoroughly satisfied.

Shane could stay in bed with her forever, at least if she were finally willing to forgive him. He knew better than to assume that all because she'd allowed him back into her bed this once that everything was back to how it had been. Molly was a different person now. They both were. Shane knew it would take more than just a fantastic night of sex to break down the walls she'd erected around her feelings for him. Tonight, however, had been a start. Shane snuggled in to cuddle with her for the night. Sadly, a peaceful end to the night was not in the cards.

THE WEAK AND THE RESTLESS

Rodney yawned, wiping his hand over his face. He repositioned himself against the brick building at his back. He was hiding in shadows like the creep everyone knew he was. Doing Maura's bidding like she was Jesus, Moses, and Mary herself.

"More like Beelzebub," he snorted to himself.

All because of his stupid, muscle head, little bro. Ax had gotten them into some things but this one. There was no turning back from this. They were Vampires, controlled by an evil bitch hell-bent on world domination. Rod had two options, die bleeding like a stuck pig or try and make a go with this half-cocked insanity. He and his brother had already died once and came damn close to it a few months back in the woods. Both times had been hell, and well, if that's where he and his bro were destined to end up, it was probably best to prolong his current situation as long as possible. Unfortunately, that meant stalking this cute, little blonde who had no idea the horrors in store for her.

Where the hell is she? She's usually home by this hour.

He flicked the end of his cigarette before putting it back between his lips. It wasn't lit since smoking would be a dead giveaway to his hideout, but it also gave him a plausible reason to be skulking about in shadows if anyone did catch him. No need to alert the human authorities that there was a Vampire war pending that hinged on the kidnapping of this one little girl.

It had been three hours since Rod had made his report to Maura, and he would surely have hell to pay for not following the "immediately" of Maura's directive. Hopefully, Ax was dulling the knife a bit with the bedroom perversions he and the She-Devil engaged in. Never in his life had Rod been so glad to fly under a woman's radar because of his less than stellar looks. At first, it had bothered Rod to see his brother so torn up and on the edge of death after each session with the mistress, but now Rod saw it as Ax finally paying for all the screwed up things he'd dragged Rod into over the years. Too bad the twisted fuck actually enjoyed it. All those years of steroid use had turned his brother into some kind of sexual sadist.

A tear rolled down his cheek. Rod would blame it on an icy wind except it wasn't quite winter and California was nowhere near as cold as his hometown in Montana. He'd say it was sweat but he never did enough exercise to even get a drop of that stuff. The only time Rod broke a sweat these days was with one look at Maura in her element.

✻✻✻

Carrie was finally over it. Her infatuation with Shane was done. She couldn't be a desperate clinger. That wasn't who she wanted to be in her new life. New Life. That had a beautiful ring to it. She was free of her father and now free of her unhealthy obsession with Shane. The new independent Carrie didn't need a man for validation.

Still, it stung as she stood there like an idiot watching Shane and Molly drive off into the sunset together.

Carrie hoped that they were able to work things out. She was no fan of Molly's, but who was she to tell Shane what was in his heart? If only it hadn't come to her complete embarrassment in front of all his friends. All in all, the party hadn't been a total wash at least until she was abandoned to the pitying stares of his friends.

"Would you like me to take you back to town?"

Carrie turned to see the newly transitioned male that had seemed so out of place all evening. Greg, if she remembered his name correctly. The brother of Gretchen, Molly's second and Claude's Mate. Carrie smirked at how quickly she applied titles to these people. They may be outcasts, but Maura's Men were more like Purebloods in their family structure than other turned Vampires.

"You move pretty well for a newly transitioned male. I don't have much experience with that, but from what I know it should take at least a year before you are capable enough to drive," Carrie said.

Greg snorted and shrugged.

"I can call you a cab if you prefer, or stay. There are plenty of rooms here for you to crash for the day," he said.

"I can't stay here," Carrie said.

During the party, Greg's stare had been worse than the others. He'd pitied her but also had the nerve to want to protect her. Carrie had noticed the way he'd circled her and Shane all evening. Careful to keep her and Molly from ever coming within arm's length of each other. He was worse than the guards her father had forced her to have as a child, but she welcomed his protection. She felt way too vulnerable in her present state. Too many old wounds rising to the surface. Poor little Carolina, always the outsider, always wanting what she can't have.

"A ride or a cab? Which is it going to be?" Greg asked.

"A ride please," Carrie whispered.

Greg led her to a black sedan without touching her. He was thankfully silent after she gave him the address of where she was staying.

"Don't take it too much to heart. Shane and Molly have a destiny that can't be changed by anyone's will but their own," he offered as she got out of the car.

Carrie just nodded. She didn't need his encouragement. In the weeks she'd known Shane he'd talked about Molly almost nonstop. It was plain as day that Molly was Shane's moon, stars, and sun. Once inside Carrie realized she wasn't in the mood to be alone. Carrie peeked out of her curtains and waited until the guy who'd driven her was gone before heading back out the door. She had no idea where she was going, but it needed to be crowded and full of energy.

❈❈❈

A car drove passed Rod's hiding spot, the headlights almost blinding in the dark of the alleyway. Luckily, Rod was far enough back that he wouldn't be seen. The car pulled up to the house he'd been watching and stopped. Rod clasped his hands together and looked up at the sky.

Finally! Date night is over. Dear whoever I'm supposed to worship as a Vampire other than Maura, please, oh please let this just be a drop-off.

The last thing Rod needed was for any of the traitors to be hanging around her place. Rod had grown stronger as a Vampire, just not as strong as those men. They had years of training and living experience on him. Not to mention his last encounters with them hadn't gone so well. If caught they would either kill him or worse torture him for information about Maura. Not that he

148

would put up a fight. If they ever got his hands on him and didn't kill him immediately, he'd dime that bitch out quicker than ink dries on paper. Thankfully, the girl bounced into her house alone. Once the car pulled off Rod would make his move.

After the car left Rod counted to ten before making a move to leave his hiding spot, but just his luck, Blondie came bounding right back out the door. He was just about to follow her down the street when he saw a familiar figure following her. It was the Boy Scout that Maura had captured for a short period of time. Even as a human he had managed to put up a good fight with Ax. Not a small feat when Ax was a man let alone now that he had Vampire strength going for him.

There was distance between the two, but Rod was going to need back up if he were going to get this girl without a fight. He followed after them, careful not to give himself away as he made the necessary calls. Blondie turned toward the fairgrounds, and Rod sighed with relief. The crowds would work in their favor. Rodney just needed Boy Scout to see who had her. No use having taken the bait and not dangling it a bit. There was no way that Rod was going to be paying any personal calls to the Traitors. That had been Declan's mistake.

❈❈❈

Greg watched as the young woman he drove home slipped back out the front door. Typical emotional female making bad decisions. He'd known Carrie wasn't just going to call it a night. She reminded him of Gretchen when she was in her teen years. Greg parked a little way down the street but with a direct view of her door. As soon as she was on her way, he got out and followed. She was much too vulnerable to be out

149

without protection. Call it a hero complex if you want, but Greg had never been able to pass up a damsel in distress.

"Fucking fabulous," Greg cursed when Carrie headed towards the fairgrounds.

It would be harder to keep track of her in the crowds of families and rowdy teens. He almost lost her twice and almost got caught a few times as well. Sure, he was following her for her own protection, but he also didn't want her to get the wrong idea about the situation. Greg wasn't interested in her in the same way Shane wasn't. Greg had unexpectedly met his destiny, and he was sure Rachel was watching his every move. At least, when she wasn't busy pulling strings to facilitate Maura's demise.

Carrie was swallowed by the crowd. Greg was just about to give up when he spotted her. She'd stopped in the middle of the fray. Her whole body stiff, her hands curled into fists as Carrie stared off in the direction opposite of him. Whatever she was looking at seemed to have made her angry but before Greg could reach her a crowd of Vampires surrounded her and then scattered leaving nothing but the hint of her perfume behind.

A deep panic began to set in as he recognized the one Vampire left standing in her place. The little weasel that worked for Maura. He eyed Greg cautiously, almost as if he were silently trying to warn him away before he turned to follow the others. He wasn't trying to be evasive. As far as Greg could tell the man was leading him to where they had taken Carrie.

Greg knew it was a trap, but there was no way he would allow Carrie to fall victim to Maura. From the stories he'd been told about Maura, there was nothing good to come. If human women were the source of her power, draining a female Vampire might be the extra rush Maura needed to make her final play. Almost as an afterthought, he decided to call for back up. He pulled out his cell and dialed Claude.

"Where are you?" His sister answered almost immediately. He chose to ignore her protectiveness this once. His baby sister, the girl who had always needed his help now acted like he was an invalid. Not that he could blame her given the circumstances, but it still grated.

"Put Claude on," Greg said.

After a minute or two, he heard Gretchen transfer the phone to her mate.

"You know you can't just run off like that. With everything that's happened and the continued threat of Maura..."

"Maura has Carrie. I'm following her henchmen right now," Greg cut Claude's lecture short.

"Carrie?" Claude asked.

"Shane's blonde friend," Greg growled.

The girl had been hanging around Shane and the mansion for the past month. No one seemed to care who or what she was other than a hindrance to Shane and Molly being together. It was something he would definitely have to talk to them about. As much as they claimed to be better people than when they were under Maura's spell, the men still had a lot of people skills to catch up on if they were going to be accepted into any kind of modern society.

"Shit! Can you stay on them—I mean, follow them, but don't get too close. We don't want you falling back into Maura's thrall. Don't hang up. Keep this line open just in case," Claude said.

Greg pocketed his phone. This confrontation with Maura had been months in the making. He only hoped that he wasn't walking right into one of Maura's grand schemes and actually had some element of surprise. He knew to wait for the others, but he also couldn't risk an innocent life. Maura couldn't and wouldn't get her hands on Carrie if he could help it.

THE BEST LAID PLANS

"Time? Time is not on anyone's side here," the Shadow screeched back.

Cat had never experienced the Shadow this out of control. Angry? Sure, but never out of control. The shadowed form paced back and forth in front of her. Like a ghost haunting the courtyard, the second place Cat had ever come across this creature.

"Look. Molly and Shane have their own demons to contend with that far exceed this week timeline you've thrown at me," Cat said as calmly as possible.

The Shadow had never done anything to really hurt Cat. With its erratic behavior now, there was no telling what may happen.

"If you had only done as I told you, that girl would be a non-issue," the Shadow spat.

Cat rolled her eyes.

"Hey! Molly has her head up her butt. That girl, her name is Carrie by the way, was a possible solution to this whole matchmaking scheme of yours. You only said that Shane needed to find love. You didn't specify it one hundred percent had to be with Molly," she said.

"Of course, I meant with Molly. This whole thing started with her, and it will end with her," the Shadow said before disappearing.

"It was so nice talking to you as always," Cat grumbled.

She pulled her cardigan tighter over her chest. There

was a sudden chill in the air that hadn't been there before. Cat went back inside, the dinner party she'd thrown in honor of Shane's progress in staying sober had been short yet eventful. The tension in the air had been so thick everyone seemed to be choking on the bad vibes. It was one of the reasons Cat had escaped to the courtyard in the first place. Molly had broken first, running away once confronted with the reality of her feelings for Shane, Shane left poor Carrie to chase after Molly, Carrie went shortly after that, and Greg left to see that Carrie got home safely before Gretchen disappeared with Claude.

As if that wasn't enough Xander had chastised her for once again meddling where she didn't belong. Of course, that led to an argument and him storming off to go hit something. Cat should have known that things were not likely to get better when she'd sought the relaxing calm of the courtyard. Too bad the Shadow interrupted her chill with crazy half-cocked accusations and demands. Always with the demands.

Another judgmental rant from the Shadow and Cat was going to explode. It had been over a year since the Shadow first appeared, and even with Claude finding love with Gretchen the atmosphere was still pretty dire. Maura still hadn't made another appearance. Xander wasn't exactly open about the investigation which pissed her off, but she knew her mate was just trying to protect her. If only he knew how deep into it she already was.

Other than the stupid necklace on her neck or the crazy shadow stalking her and torturing her best friend, Cat's heart was very much in this fight as well. She'd come to think of all the men as her family and Gretchen too. She even found herself checking on Gretchen's brother, Greg, from time to time. Having gone through an unwanted change, she knew how isolating those first few months could feel. Adjusting to your newfound strengths and weaknesses.

However, that wasn't what was pressing at the moment. Cat had to find a way to get Molly and Shane back together. It was a start that they had left the dinner party together even if it meant an awkward moment with Carrie.

Cat began to clear the glasses of blood left around the room. Some dinner party when all the courses were liquid. She hated to waste it considering the source but once warmed the blood would be rancid in a few hours. She headed for the kitchen only to be nearly knocked over by a half-naked Claude.

"Hey! Where's Xander?" he asked pulling a black t-shirt over his sinfully defined abs.

"Wrecking shit out back. What's going on?" Cat asked.

"Carrie's been taken," he called out as he ran towards the backyard.

Cat nearly dropped the glasses in her hands as the reality of his words sunk in. No wonder the Shadow had been acting strangely. Shane had lost his shit when Molly had died. Even though he wasn't romantically interested in Carrie, she was still an innocent caught in the crosshairs because of him. Cat ran into the house to change into more fight friendly clothes. It didn't matter what Xander or the others said. They were going to need the help tonight. Speaking of help. Cat pulled out her phone and dialed Molly. Carrie was probably the last person Molly would ever want to save, but this would be the best chance they all had of getting rid of Maura once and for all.

Cat still remembered how her friend had managed to save them all during the last encounter, and she knew Molly and her powers would be needed tonight. She just hoped she wasn't interrupting anything good between Molly and Shane.

✳✳✳

"You want me to what," Molly screeched.

As it was Molly was already pissed that Shane had left her bed for that girl, and now her best friend was demanding she come and save her. Well, not just the girl but Xander and Claude, Shane too.

"Look, forget whatever is going on with you and Shane! Molly, this is way bigger than that. We all would have died if you hadn't saved us the last time, and from all the evidence the men have gathered, Maura is stronger this time. Way stronger and with an army of men instead of just the two barely transitioned thugs we fought the first time," Cat said.

Molly crossed her arms over her chest and glanced between Cat and Gretchen. Both of them standing nervously and ready for action. Like at any moment they would grab her and drag her away with them if she continued to refuse. The situation wasn't ideal. Molly could care less if Maura drained every drop of that bitch who'd tried to displace her in Shane's heart. It was tempting to let the dice fall as they may. The problem was that also meant putting her friend's lives at risk.

"Fine," she grumbled, "but only for the sake of your mates and my own desire for revenge on that psycho."

Cat smirked before taking Molly's arm and guiding her to the door.

"I'm glad you made the right decision," Cat said.

"Thank you," Gretchen sighed, her shoulders sagging with relief but still tense with worry over the men in her life.

156

Unlike Cat and Molly, Gretchen stood to lose the most in this fight. Not only was Claude in danger but Gretchen's brother, Greg, was the first at the scene. That didn't bode well for him so fresh from his turning. He was the most at risk of falling under Maura's spell. Especially since she was his sire. Molly knew all too well how Maura's powers of persuasion could rob anyone of their common sense. Make them do anything for her, even turn them against their own family.

"Don't thank me. I can't even guarantee me being there will help," she said.

Molly glanced again at her best friend, tears welling in her eyes. Molly wasn't entirely sure she'd ever genuinely apologized to Cat for that awful night. She'd been an idiot. That drastic move, so out of character for Molly, brought to light the evil that Maura represented. Molly took a steady calming breath. Molly needed to stay calm and aloof if she was going to get through this night. The few times her powers had emerged had been during times of great emotional peril and stress. If Molly had any chance at controlling it, she needed to be thinking clearly.

❁❁❁

Xander, Claude, and Shane strapped on as many weapons as they could physically carry. The last they'd heard from Greg was that Maura had indeed amassed an army. Shane just hoped the poor man was alright. Shane had used his laptop to help with tracking Greg to the warehouse district, but that was where the signal had been terminated.

"I heard some metal clanging in the background before the line went dead. It would make sense that the gym over there is our target," Claude said nodding to the only lit building on the street.

157

"Even so we need to be careful. I know Greg could be in grave danger, but he could also already be dead. We don't want to run in blind," Xander said.

"I'll take the front door. I'm the least intimidating of us if Claude is wrong. It's also my fault that Carrie was caught up in all this, so I should be the one taking that risk," Shane said.

His friends just stared at him for a moment before looks of pride crossed their faces. Xander gave Shane a pat on the back before taking off towards the rear of the warehouse.

"I'm glad to see you've grown some balls in therapy. Just try not to get yourself killed before we even get to see that bitches face," Claude said before taking off as well.

Shane would have taken the man's jabs as an insult if he hadn't known Claude for as long as he had. Claude was always the first to throw stones instead of facing his emotions. Even his relationship with Gretchen hadn't changed that aspect of his personality. He waited until his friends were in position before he strode towards the door. He placed one hand on the knob and gripped the pistol on his hip with the other. He'd be lying if he said he didn't feel ready to piss his pants.

Shane was no warrior. He'd been trained in combat skills out of necessity, but that didn't make his decision any less harrowing. He shook his head. It wasn't just his life at stake. Carrie was in there as a prisoner, Greg was also there and likely dead or worse. Shane would never be redeemed in the eyes of his family if he showed the colors of a coward when they needed him most.

"One, two...." The door swung open before he could finish his count, and the weasel-faced man from before stood in the doorway.

The man smirked at Shane and stepped aside as if he

were inviting him in for dinner.

"Glad you could make it in such a timely manner. I've dispatched as many as I could, but the rest is up to you, brother."

Shane was confused. He stepped inside to see a room full of dead bodies. Piles of unmarked flesh laying across every piece of equipment the only evidence of foul play were the sickly scent of poison coming from the cups and bottles of blood. Only new Vampires were susceptible to poisoning and only by nightshade.

"Thank you," Shane muttered.

His relief was short lived as a guttural scream could be heard from the office above.

"You go ahead up. I'll clean up here and let the others out back in," the man said.

He began to lug the massive bodies into a pile close to the stove in the corner. Shane whistled softly. The signal for Claude and Xander to make their move. The men burst in through the back and side entrance but paused when they took in the sight before them.

"What the hell," Claude cursed while Xander turned his sword on the weasel almost immediately.

"Hey! I'm Rod. Sorry for, uh, the last time, but you know well my predicament. I just want out like you guys. I took care of these monsters, but the real monster is upstairs with your friends," Rod rambled.

Xander lowered his weapon slightly but didn't take his eyes off of Rod.

"I don't like this," Xander whispered.

Claude nodded in agreement.

"I'll go upstairs. If this is a trap you will both know soon enough," Shane volunteered.

❋❋❋

The ride to the warehouse district was tense and

159

quiet. So deep in their own heads, none of the women uttered a peep. When they arrived at the spot where the men's GPS trackers indicated, the scene was underwhelming and frightening all at once. It was dark and eerily quiet. The only light coming from a single street lamp two buildings down. Barely enough light to pierce the darkness of the moonless night. They had pulled up right next to Claude's blacked out SUV. Neither he nor the others were inside it which meant they had already made their move. The girls had no idea if they were inside or even which warehouse could possibly be Maura's hideout.

"Did you bring any weapons?" Molly asked.

Cat shot her a glare before opening the trunk. Molly peered inside and rolled her eyes when all she saw were two measly fencing swords and a crossbow. Thank god she at least had a decent sized pocket knife and a handful of sharpened wood pencils in her purse. As the female owner of a nightclub, Molly kept odd hours and had to be alert. Granted her Vampire strength was enough to overpower most human men. Most Vampires were afraid of her solely because she was the only female ever sired by Maura. Molly didn't take either for granted. If the incident had taught her anything, it was to be prepared for the worst at all cost. Still, her self-defense precautions wouldn't be much help. Good for a handful of assailants if they came at her one at a time and she had the element of surprise but not at all helpful if she was swarmed by an army.

Gretchen grabbed the crossbow and Cat grabbed the swords. She tried to hand one to Molly, but she shook her head.

"I don't know how to use a sword! I'm more likely to cut my own head off instead of someone else's, and I am not going through that shit again," Molly snapped.

Cat rolled her eyes before tucking the other sword into a holster she apparently had hidden under her jacket. Molly saw Gretchen tucking arrows in a sling before tossing it onto her shoulder.

"I know you are super powerful and shit, but I swear to god if my brother and Claude die because you were too proud to ask for weapons training, I will make your life a living hell," she spat.

Normally, Molly would go on the defense in a situation like this, but there really weren't situations like this. She had been too proud to ask for training of any kind from Xander or anyone for that matter. At least for anything other than the Council, and even then, it was only because according to the Council she had been under Xander's jurisdiction as one of Maura's cursed and untrustworthy turns. Just the thought of the Council made Molly cringe. Well, not the Council, just Maximus, the pureblood representative. He gave her all sorts of hell no feelings.

"Alright let's go," Gretchen said moving away from the car.

"Hold on we need to have a plan. We don't even know where to go," Molly said.

Gretchen paused and straightened, agitation written all over her body.

"All the buildings are dark except for that one three doors down. That should be our first stop," Gretchen said.

"Fine, but you just want to walk in the front door?" Molly asked.

"Look we know the men are here. My brother has been here. They would have gone in there by now," Gretchen said.

"We don't even know if that is where they are," Molly yelled in frustration.

"Shhh! Both of you calm down. Gretchen is right, it's worth a look. My weapons are concealed, and I'm the least likely to be recognized by Maura or her minions, so I'll go in first. I'll walk in. If it's a normal warehouse, I'll walk right back out. If not then you two will be right there," Cat said.

Molly was seriously regretting the decision to follow her friend's insistence that she come along with them. Even the first time, before she'd known about her powers, had been easier than this. A lone cabin in the woods was a lot more obvious than a warehouse with its lights on when everything else was dark. Hell, a lot of Vampires didn't even use lights because of their sensitive vision. This was a long shot, a serious long shot.

"This is stupid. We should call the guys. If they are inside, they won't answer. If they are a safe distance away, they will give us some indication of where to go," Molly tried to reason with the two women who were the sum total of those she considered family.

"If they don't answer they could be seriously hurt, and if they do? Well, you know they will make us go home. They wouldn't accept our help in this," Cat said.

"Pretty sure they didn't ask for your help in the first place so no harm no foul," Molly said and picked up her phone.

She found Xander's number in her recent contacts and hit dial. It rung four times before Molly frowned and hung up.

"I guess we're going in," Cat said and marched off before Molly could stop her.

✻✻✻

Brody checked his phone again. Molly's cell phone was no longer pinging at her home. Instead, it looked to be heading to the warehouse district.

"I know where they are headed, sir," he said looking up at Maximus who sat anxiously at the other end of the SUV.

"It's about damn time! They better have my daughter, and she better be safe," the man snarled.

It didn't take long for the driver to change course. The warehouse district wasn't very large. They cruised each block until finding the discarded vehicle of the exiles. Brody recognized it from his few encounters with the men around town. They parked on a different block to be on the safe side. Maximus was practically climbing out of the vehicle before it had stopped.

"Sir, I suggest you let us take the lead on this. There is no telling what we may encounter," The head of the Council's security force said.

Maximus didn't care what the man thought. He was here for his daughter and nothing else. Those devil spawns were dead meat as far as he was concerned. Brody was glad the man was focusing his ire on the situation and not on the fact that he hadn't been able to deliver Carolina to him unharmed as promised. They'd gone to the condo she'd rented and then to the mansion where Maura's Men stayed. They hadn't been allowed entrance. He had to give the men credit. Their human security was immune to even Maximus's power of influence. That kind of paranoia was impressive yet warranted in their case.

If it weren't for Molly leaving on the location services on her phone, Brody likely would have been killed on the spot. Maximus wasn't a patient man, especially when it came to the well-being of his precious Carolina. At this point Brody wasn't even sure the spoiled brat was worth the hassle. If she wanted to live her life as an exile that was on her. It was a waste to be sure, but at this point, Brody was willing to move on.

"Fine, but I'm not just going to sit here and wait. I have not reached the position I have without skill in battle," Maximus huffed.

The head of security sighed but nodded in acquiescence. Arguing with a pureblood wasn't in his best interest, even if it meant possibly leading the man into a trap. Brody on the other hand would much rather stay in the car. He was not battle hardened. Sure, he could be ruthless in politics and the boardroom, but hand to hand combat had never tickled his fancy. The scout they had sent returned with more detailed news of the men's whereabouts. After the Head of Security called for backup, he motioned for the small contingent they already had to get ready to move.

"I can stay out here and make sure no one slips by," Brody offered.

"If you want to mate my daughter you better be prepared to fight for her. I will not have a pansy mated into my family," Maximus spat.

Brody nodded and stifled a groan as he slid from the leather seats and out into the cool night. He took a look around as the security force prepared for action. Even with three cars full of heavily armed and trained vampires, Brody couldn't help but feel his life was about to end in a most heinous fashion.

There had to be a way out of this debacle. Brody might have to go inside but that didn't mean he had to be the first one in. He would stay behind with Maximus to wait for the rest of their back up, and if things got hairy, it would be easy for him to slip away unnoticed and hopefully unscathed. Brody had come this far in his little game. All it would take was a little more effort for his goal to be realized. It was too close to give up now.

"Alright, let's move," the head of security called out. "Remember they are all under order of death, even the women," Maximus cried as they moved forward.

FIRE AND BRIMSTONE

Maura stood over the two men battling for life and honor at her feet. She couldn't hold back the smile that crept to her lips at the sight as they tore into each other. Blood flowing freely from the men's open wounds. The pureblood bitch was whimpering in a panic over the state of her would-be rescuer, and that made the moment even sweeter. Maura had missed having a show before her feast. It was like the old days when she'd lived in Rome. Two gladiators fighting to the death at their master's command.

This pittance of an office was far from the grandeur and spectacle of the Colosseum, but it was the closest she would get in this day and age. Axel and Gregory were locked in a heated battle. Nothing was off limits as they pummeled each other. Maura was almost sad that Gregory would have to die at the end of this, no matter who reigned victorious at the end. He was a magnificent fighter, his muscles rolled delectably under taut skin as he moved with practiced ease. His attacks were graceful and deadly whereas Axel relied on brute strength and opportunity.

The girl chained at Maura's side strained at her bonds, screaming around the ball gag, shoved between small lips. Her lips were beginning to crack at the edges, the scent of her blood wafting up to Maura. It was all Maura could do not to take from the girl already. Her pure blood was just what she needed to revive her strength. There was a hint of magic in the girl's blood as well. Something that would only be possible if she fed on a magic wielder. In the years since her resurrection, Maura had searched for the people who had given her the tools to become the woman she was and had found no trace of them.

They'd gone underground after the persecution of both human and undead alike. Where they'd gone? Maura had no idea, but with this new development, perhaps their fate was worse than she expected. To be a blood slave was a worse fate than death itself. Maura knew that from experience. It was one of the reasons she made sure to take every last drop from her victims. Not just to ensure her beauty was sustained but also to make sure they could never be used again.

Axel and Gregory tumbled forward, closer to Maura and her bait. Maura looked up at the door. What was taking those idiots so long? She had left the man's phone operational for long enough. They should have been able to track them.

"I guess you mean less to Shane than even you thought," Maura spat at the girl who was proving to be even more useless as bait as she was for entertainment.

"Maybe I'll throw Axel a bone once he finishes with your guard. I'm sure he has lots of pent-up anger ready to be spent on the tender likes of you."

That got Axel's attention. The man's gaze went from murderous to lustful as he gazed on his would-be pride. Too bad it also took his eyes away from his opponent. Seizing the opportunity, Gregory grabbed one of Maura's discarded toys and shoved it through Axel's abdomen. Axel screamed in agony before falling to the floor in a heap. He was not dead yet, but he would be soon after Maura was done with the traitors. If they ever arrived, that is. Gregory charged at Maura, but she caught him by the neck.

He may have won the battle, but he unquestionably was no match for her. She tossed him against the brick wall, his head smacking it with a satisfying thud before he slid to the ground. She would have her fun with him later. She was done waiting for the others. She would have her prize now and dangle the purebloods exsanguinated body from the flagpole out front. A symbol of the traitor's failure and the return of Maura to power.

❋❋❋

Shane entered the room just as Maura was about to strike. Jumping into action, Shane pulled the trigger on the gun in his hand. The bullets landing in Maura's arm. She hissed, dropping Carrie to the ground.

"It's about time you showed up," Maura growled.

Shane hated the way his body froze under her direct glare. It was as if it hadn't been years since she'd ruled his world. His hand was still outstretched, his gun pointed at her head instead of her arm, but he couldn't pull the trigger. It was as if there was a miscommunication between his brain and his limbs. His fingers refused to work, but his legs moved him closer and closer to the devil.

Shane was hopeless. Any thought of redemption for his past cowardice was long gone as Maura reached out to him. Shane vaguely heard a commotion erupt downstairs. The sound of metal clashing upon metal and the unmistakable zing of a bow let Shane know he wasn't going to be receiving his friends help before it was too late. Maura grabbed both Shane and Carrie by the neck and carried them towards the sounds of battle. Apparently, Shane's surrender wasn't enough,

Maura wanted an audience.

Shane was unprepared for what came into view once Maura stood out on the stair ledge. The scene below was perplexing, to say the least. Xander and Claude fought back-to-back, fending off not just muscled Vampires but Council security forces. The weasel of a man stood by the pile of poisoned men and watched with glee as one by one they rose and joined the fight. Of course, it had been a trap all along. They had known it, and Shane had fallen for it. Dooming himself and his friends to lengthy battle that could only end with their demise.

Maura was distracted by the chaos beneath. So distracted she hadn't noticed Greg stirring in the room behind them. Shane only saw because his drooping head was positioned at just the right angle to see the door as well as the carnage below. Shane wanted to warn Gregory to stay down. To pretend he was dead until the worst had passed. Maybe even make an escape from the small window, but he couldn't. Not without giving the man away to Maura.

Greg stood in the doorway, and Shane lolled his head to the side. Doing his best to indicate that he should save Carrie if he could. Shane was already a lost cause. He could feel Maura's pull seeping into his consciousness. Shane knew it was only a matter of time before he was entirely enthralled. Greg nodded as if he understood. In one quick movement, Greg grabbed Carrie's waist while throwing his body into Maura. The move sent all of them tumbling over the rail.

❈❈❈

The look on Cat's face when she opened the door to the gym was enough to send Molly into a dead sprint.

Cat had already run inside her sword in hand by the time Molly got there, and what she saw gave her pause. The room was filled with dueling Vampires, but that wasn't what had Molly stunned like a statue by the door. Greg had just thrown himself into Maura sending himself and her plummeting to the floor below. Not just her but also Shane and the bitch Carrie. The sight of Shane in danger had her powers surfacing in an instant, but Molly held back.

It was too soon to tell if she would need them again and as far as she knew it was a single shot kind of weapon. It was best Molly save the fatal blast for Maura, even as it killed her to hear the sickening crunch of bodies hitting the pavement. Those involved would be grievously injured but not dead. Instead, she moved along the walls of the room. No one seemed to pay her any mind as they battled. One of Gretchen's arrows skimmed Molly's cheek on the way to its intended target.

The weasel of the man who had helped Maura at the cabin. It hit him squarely in the forehead but didn't penetrate deep enough to do anything but annoy the Vampire. He swatted the arrow from its perch before stalking towards the stairs. The massive pile of bodies he'd been standing by was finally depleted. The muscled Vampires shaking off whatever stupor they were in to join the ranks of the already battling masses.

Bodies were dropping like flies as her friends battled valiantly, both aided and attacked by the Council forces. Molly had no idea where they had come from or why they were even there. Maura was a threat to them for sure, but there had been no mobilizing of forces rumored about amongst the Vampire population. No indication that the Council had any more idea of Maura's whereabouts than any of them had. Of course,

Xander could have raised the alarm to them, but that still didn't give them enough time to mobilize this caliber of forces.

This whole scene felt off to Molly. It didn't take her long to realize why. The last of Maura's new army was already being stricken down. Her friends had circled into each other, breathing heavily and battle weary, but their fight wasn't over. The Council forces still advanced until they were all trapped against the fallen pile that was Maura and Shane. Carrie and Greg were nowhere to be seen. Molly wasn't sure if they had fallen further away or if they had somehow managed to recover more quickly and slip away. Either scenario was good for Molly at the moment. That was two fewer people to worry about as one of the Council soldiers whispered into his wrist. A minute later Maximus came strolling in with Brody in tow. Both men looking regal and unfazed by the gore squishing under their feet.

The Council forces parted upon their arrival allowing for Maximus to step through and face off with Xander and the others.

"You've proved yourselves in league with this wench. I will have all of your heads before the night is over," Maximus barked out.

Claude rolled his eyes as he settled into a new battle stance.

"Go ahead and try old man. We took out Maura once. You will be a picnic," he snarled, and Molly stifled a laugh.

Of course, Claude wouldn't think twice about insulting a member of the Council. It was why Xander was in charge of dealing with the Council. Claude lacked tact, and Shane lacked the warrior background to be taken seriously.

Words were exchanged between her friends and the

two men but in all of that none of them saw Maura stirring behind them. Molly herself hadn't noticed until it was too late. She saw Maura slowly stand, her mouth moving as an enchantment spilled from her lips. The temperature in the room went up at least fifty degrees in a matter of minutes. A wall of shimmering light encompassed the entire group. Molly ran forward only to bounce off the force field like it was a balloon. She stood and tried again, banging with her fists as those inside the bubble began to sink to the ground, grabbing at their throats, eyes bulging from their sockets. A few of them even had raised boils as if they were being suffocated and boiled alive at the same time.

Now was the time to act. Now was the time for Molly to use her powers but nothing would come. She focused as best she could. Nothing happened to her. Not even a tingle until she saw Carrie standing on the other end of the bubble. Shane was awake now too, but he wasn't looking at Molly. Shane was standing in front of Carrie as she cried. He pressed his hand to hers through the barrier. Power surged within Molly instantly. She broke through the barrier, seething with rage. Molly stormed towards Shane and Carrie, but Maura got in her path.

"I'll be taking what's mine," Maura growled lunging forward.

She grabbed the necklace from Cat's limp body and pressed it to Molly's chest. Molly could feel the power draining from her body and into the necklace. She could see the light transforming within the stone, turning dark and menacing before traveling into Maura. The barrier began to close again. Molly was trapped inside now. Her light and life were leeching into the necklace being pressed into her chest. Instead of fire, she felt ice, slithering into her chest, wrapping around her heart and choking the blood flow.

Molly's eyes never left Shane as he tried to comfort Carrie even in his dying breath. Molly shook her head. This couldn't be the end. Not this, not when she had just found love again with Shane. They couldn't die like this. With him comforting the woman who had nearly torn them apart forever. Maura couldn't win this fight. Not after the horrors, she'd inflicted on everyone Molly had come to love. A savage roar built in Molly's lungs before erupting forth from her mouth.

It startled Maura, causing her to step back. As soon as the necklace was off her chest, her powers swelled, melting the ice in her chest and spreading through her body. Molly felt flames creeping over her skin, not painful to her but when she grabbed Maura's arm, it charred the demon's skin as quickly as a flame to paper. Maura screamed and tried to wrench away, but it was too late. Molly pulled the woman to her holding her tight. To anyone else, it would seem a hug between old friends if it weren't for Maura's agonized screams.

"Rot in hell, bitch," Molly whispered in Maura's ear even as she directed her glare at Carrie.

Molly used her anger and jealousy to fuel the intense emotion needed to maintain the spell she had over Maura. The stench of burning flesh filled Molly's nostrils, but she didn't let go until Maura's body withered into a pile of ash at her feet. At least the Shadow's torment had been good for something. She wouldn't have been able to hold on as long as was necessary if it hadn't been for her familiarity with the sickly-sweet smell.

The necklace had still been in Maura's hands when Molly had burned her alive. Now it was not but a pile of ash along with its master. With Maura vanquished, her spell vanished, but the effects lingered. The men around her coughed and gasped for air. Those who had suffered boils were healing slowly. The room was thick with residual magic, and Molly welcomed it into her body. Using it to replace the energy she'd lost in the use of her own spell.

"Molly," Shane's voice cut into her thoughts before his body was flush against her.

"Don't you have a girlfriend to attend to?" Molly asked, and Shane nodded.

"Yes, and she is here in my arms," he said before kissing her senseless.

Molly kissed him back. She shot a dirty look Carrie's way before closing her eyes and reveling in the love between her and Shane. Molly was petty, and she knew it. She belonged to Shane. He belonged to her. Her jealousy would be something she would have to address later.

"I hate to interrupt, but we should get going before Maximus wakes and orders his men to decapitate us. I was up for the fight before. Now I'd much rather be home bedding my mate," Claude said.

Shane shot him a glare but guided Molly out the door anyway. It was best they left now. After tonight there would be no hiding from the Council. Molly's powers were no longer a rumor but a fact. They needed to regroup before that hammer fell upon them. Gretchen and Claude rode in Claude's SUV with Greg and Carrie, while Shane and Molly slid in the backseat of Cat's vehicle. Xander, of course, chose to drive. Molly didn't blame him. Even after the incident that had taken Molly's life, Cat was still a reckless driver prone to fits of rage at the slightest perceived misstep of other drivers.

❈❈❈

Brody stood stalk still. His chest heaving as he sucked in air and tried to calm his nerves. It was deadly silent in the room below. The crackling energy of dueling magic had faded, but he was terrified of the outcome. It was only by chance that he'd slipped away before the sphere of death enclosed everyone but himself and Molly. Brody couldn't be sure, but maybe Carrie and another man had escaped it as well. Honestly, he didn't care. At the moment he was safe.

A groan sounded nearby. Brody forced his eyes to open. He wasn't in a closet as he had thought. He was in an office or rather a torture chamber. There was a desk there. The sturdy sort. Not unusual until he noticed it was covered in scratches and gauges, and stained so red with blood that the recipient of whatever had occurred couldn't possibly still be alive. Vampire or not. He winced as he glanced around and saw the barbaric tools hung along the wall behind it.

As a young Vampire, he'd heard stories about Maura's sadistic tendencies, but he hadn't imagined that being one of Maura's Men could have been so bad. He was no stranger to rough play, but the display before him was far beyond any of that. The groan came again, and a shifting figure at his side caught his attention.

Brody's hand flew up to his mouth to keep from vomiting as he witnessed a bull of a man tear a massive spiked weapon from his abdomen. Blood and guts spilling to the already gore slick floor. Brody didn't have time to register anything more as the man lurched forward in a supposed attack only to fall forward. The man lay there choking on his own blood, suffocating on his own organs as he had face planted right into them.

Brody realized he had to be one of Maura's army. He wasn't quite dead yet. If by some stroke of luck Maura hadn't killed everyone downstairs, Brody would be known as a legend in his own right for taking down one of her progeny. That thought bolstered his courage. Brody carefully walked forward, picking up the discarded weapon and lifted it high over his head. All it would take was one blow to sever the man's spine and put an end to his misery. An end to his suffering and a beginning to Brody's glory.

He swung his arm down with a guttural scream. The weapon slamming onto the man's head instead of his neck as Brody had planned. Brody yanked at the weapon, but it was lodged in the nearly dead man's skull. Brody bent down to the man to see if maybe the blow had been enough. Unfortunately, he could still hear the gurgling coming from the man's chest. Brody stood again. He tugged and tugged, but the weapon wouldn't budge. He tried wiggling it out but only succeeded in splashing massive amounts of blood and gore on his bespoke suit. Probably not the best attire for this sort of thing, but Brody hadn't planned on going to battle.

Frustrated, he kicked the dying man before trying one last time to pull the weapon free. All he needed was one more good swing and the glory of the night would be his. He pulled with all his might and finally the weapon came free. Brody stumbled back as it dislodged, his oxfords not able to find footing on the blood-slicked floor. He did his best to catch his balance but ended up falling on his ass. The weapon slipping from his grasp and landing on his leg, embedding in his flesh.

Brody howled in pain. He lay there for a moment before starting to laugh. It would be a better story now with a war wound. No one would believe he bested one of Maura's Men without injury. That is if Maura had been defeated. If not, well he may as well have died with the rest of the lot.

✢✢✢

Rodney watched the man who'd dealt the final blow

to his brother from behind the massive desk. Rodney had come up to see if his brother was still alive only to be interrupted by this asshole. The Council's liaison, Brody, was even more of a prick than Rodney thought. Maura was dead. Rodney had felt almost immediately when her hold on him and his brother had been released. Rodney was a free man. If only he could get out of this godforsaken place undetected.

Brody lay there laughing like a lunatic and that pissed Rodney off. His brother was lying in a pool of his own blood and guts, stuck in the limbo between life and death because he was a fucking Vampire. He would lie there suffering until the last drop of blood left his body. There was nothing Rodney could do for him at this point. Yet another massive weight off his shoulders. Rodney was beholden to no one at this point. Still, it didn't sit right with him that this man hadn't had the decency to finish the job. That Brody was content to lay there without ending things mercifully. He deserved to die too.

Rodney gathered his strength and rose from behind his hiding place. He didn't have much time before the Vampires he heard below would come to check things out. Rodney snatched a fireplace poker from the wall and stalked over to his target. He would dispatch Brody and get the hell out before he got caught. He would still be considered a threat by the others. They wouldn't think twice before slicing and dicing him like the rest of Maura's army.

It took a moment for Brody to notice Rodney's approach. The man stopped laughing, and his eyes widened in fear. Rodney could feel his lips curling over his fangs. He was right there, so close but when Rodney's arms swung down, the blow didn't hit Brody. Instead, there was a sickening crunch as Rodney severed Axel's spinal cord. His brother could finally rest in peace.

Breathing heavily, Rodney sank to his knees next to his brother's still body. He roared in rage and pain. His body shook with racking sobs. He'd killed his own brother. His baby brother. Maura had succeeded in making him just as much a monster as she was.

The door opened then, and Rodney looked up. A man dressed in black tactical gear stood in the doorway weapon drawn and ready. Rodney didn't make a move. Didn't open his mouth to protest as the man pulled the trigger. A searing pain tore through his chest. Rodney collapsed on top of his brother, his body draping over Axel in the same protective way it used to when their father would beat them. A fitting end to their story. Rodney protecting him in death as in life.

ONE DOOR CLOSES

Greg saw Rachel slip down the hall toward his room as soon as he entered the mansion. He was tired and badly injured, but seeing her made him forget all of that. Now that the threat was gone, he wanted to have a serious talk with her.

If you had told him a few months ago that he'd be living his life hidden away as a newly turned Vampire, hunted by an evil Vampiress, and in love with a ghost? He'd have questioned your sanity. Now it was par for the course. He longed to lay with Rachel this evening. Maybe he could convince her to finally give in to the pent-up tension between them. Sure, they touched, nothing sexual just innocent hand-holding, but Greg wanted more.

He wanted Rachel. She was his light on the darkest days. Today certainly qualified as one of those days. Greg marched toward his room with barely a word to anyone else. Not that it mattered. Gretchen was already swept into Claude's arms and being carried up the stairs. Claude no doubt had the same intentions for his sister tonight as he did with Rachel. He didn't like to think about that, but he could understand the man at least. Cat and Xander had just pulled up, and Cat was already leading Carrie safely away before Molly even caught a glimpse of the woman.

As soon as Greg entered his room, he swept Rachel into his arms, kissing her like he had dreamed about so many nights. She swooned and relaxed into his embrace. Accepting his kiss with eagerness before pulling away.

"Greg, please! Don't make this any harder. I cannot stay long. I just had to see you one last time before..." Rachel didn't finish her sentence.

Greg was noticing for the first time that her presence wasn't as clear as before. It was as if a dense fog obscured her visage.

"No! You can't leave like this. Not now. I love you," Greg said, and she smiled sadly before floating back into his arms.

"Kiss me one last time. Kiss me and promise you will find someone worthy of your love," she said.

She was fading faster, turning into nothing more than a shadow before his eyes. He kissed her with all the passion he had inside him. Her pliant lips became nothing but a wisp of smoke.

"Promise me," her voice sounded a million miles away.

"Don't make me," Greg choked up.

"Promise."

Her voice barely a whisper now. The shadow Rachel had transformed into was fading.

"I promise," he said, but there was nothing left to promise to.

Rachel was gone.

❈❈❈

"You can sleep in here tonight," Cat said, showing Carrie into a nice room off one of the three hallways in the mansion.

To think she'd been here just a few hours before getting her heart crushed and now, she was just glad to be alive. Her heart was still racing from the near-death experience. Not only had her life been threatened by Maura who was now thankfully no more, but she had a feeling Molly wasn't going to just ignore her presence in town. Carrie had been around long enough to know that Molly was well on her way to becoming a significant player in Vampire society, and to top it all off, she was a magic wielder.

Sure, Carrie had some protection as a born Vampire and a member of the ruling family, but the look Molly shot her before Shane had swept her into a passionate kiss was more than enough warning. Carrie pulled out her phone and sent a message to her father. She didn't want him storming their mansion tonight in his impatience to have her home safe. She would leave first thing in the morning. She would go to the magistrate tomorrow and face her father's wrath. Something that was suddenly less scary in comparison. She had lost Shane, but that was something she could live with. Losing her life was a whole other matter. Besides, almost dying had given her a new appreciation for her father's protective streak. Having round the clock bodyguards didn't seem like that bad of a deal any longer.

Maybe she shouldn't have slipped away before her father's men had a chance to spirit her away. There was nothing left for her here but terrible memories of failure. Carrie was a failure in love and a failure in life. Carrie cuddled up on the too soft mattress of the guest bed and closed her eyes. She probably wouldn't get much sleep, but she could try at least. Carrie was just beginning to relax when there was a knock on the door. For a minute she considered just pretending that she was sleeping already, but in a household full of Vampires it would be obvious that she wasn't.

She got up and opened the door, half expecting an irate Molly ready to finish the job, but instead it was

Greg. He looked exhausted, and bruises were sprouting around his left eye and cheek. He'd taken a beating on her behalf, and she hated seeing him still suffering.

"Greg? Come inside," she said and pulled him into the room closing the door.

"I just wanted to check on you. After the night you had. I didn't think you'd feel comfortable alone," he said, but there was something else in his tone besides worry.

He seemed sad, and she had a feeling it had something to do with the Shadowy figure she'd seen him disappear with earlier. Maybe it was Greg who needed to be with someone right now. She wasn't about to turn him away. He was just as much responsible for saving her life as any of the others. More so because if he hadn't followed her when she'd foolishly left her apartment, no one would have known she was in trouble in the first place.

"A girl could be better, but you need to rest and to feed. You are in too much pain," she said sitting next to him on the bed.

Without really thinking about it she tilted her head to the side and offered him her neck. As a born Vampire female, it was taboo of her to do so with anyone other than her mate. Yet at the moment she didn't care. He would heal much faster if he drank from her, propriety be damned. He had done more than enough to earn the privilege of her vein.

Greg eyed her for a moment as if unsure of what to do, but she knew exactly when his instinct took over. His eyes darkening before he descended upon her. No one had ever taken from her vein before. She'd anticipated it hurting a little. Instead, Carrie was surprised by the jolt of arousal that shot from his bite to her genitals. Each pull of his mouth translating into a pulsing between her thighs. Carrie couldn't help the moan that escaped her lips or the whimper of disappointment as he immediately pulled away at the sound.

"I'm so sorry. I shouldn't have," Greg said.

He moved away from Carrie with a look of disgust on his face. Greg made a move for the door, but Carrie grabbed his arm.

"Don't be sorry. Please stay," Carrie whispered.

Her need overriding her common sense.

Their eyes locked, bodies tense with unspoken desire. Greg wanted her; it was evident in the molten slate of Greg's gaze. Carrie's heart beat rapidly in her chest. Faster even than when she'd been faced by certain death. She struggled to keep her breathing even. Doing her best not to seem as desperate as she felt.

"I can't. I'm in love with someone else. I mean she's gone now, but it's still too soon," Greg said.

Carrie let her hand fall from his arm. Of course, that was apparently her type, unavailable men.

"Oh, I didn't... I'm sorry," Carrie said.

Greg knelt in front of her making sure to maintain eye contact.

"Thank you for sharing your blood with me. I really just wanted to make sure you were okay," Greg said.

"It's fine. I'm fine, thank you. You can go," Carrie said, though part of her wanted to beg Greg to stay.

He brushed a soft kiss across her forehead, innocent and sweet before leaving her alone in the room. She fell back on the bed with a frustrated groan before tears she hadn't known she was holding began to stream down her face. Her body may have survived this night, but her heart surely hadn't. She clearly needed to evaluate her choice in men.

❈❈❈

"You didn't have to do that. You didn't need to put

183

yourself at risk like that," Shane said taking Molly's hand in his.

Tears streamed down her face as she shook her head.

"Yes, I did! I couldn't lose you, not to her," Molly sobbed.

Shane pulled her into his arms. Molly hated that it had come to this. That it had taken nearly losing everyone she'd come to care about before she'd realized there was no way she could live without Shane. For once her crazy powers had come in handy freeing her family, and they were her family, from Maura once and for all. Shane pulled back a little and kissed her.

"You could never lose me. Even if I had died back there, I would always be with you. I love you, and nothing will ever keep me from you again," Shane said.

He kissed Molly again. She melted into him, letting her emotions flow from her lips to his. The kiss was innocent enough at first, but it became more frenzied and passionate as he pressed her against the wall.

"We should probably go to your room," Molly gasped breaking out of her lust fueled stupor long enough to realize they could be interrupted at any moment by the other occupants of the mansion.

Not that it was likely. Molly was sure Cat and Gretchen were thoroughly occupied by their mates at the moment. That still left Gretchen's brother and that little slut Carrie. Just the thought of the woman who'd tried to steal Shane from her shifted Molly's mood.

"Good idea," Shane said not sensing the change.

He grabbed her hand and pulled her down the hall to his room. It was different than she remembered. It had been modernized at some point during their separation. Molly hated to think that Carrie had held any part in the redecoration of this place. Finally aware of Molly's lack of interest in his advances, Shane pulled back and made her look at him.

"What's wrong love," he asked.

Molly took a deep breath.

"Did she help you with this," she asked.

He chuckled softly before kissing her.

"So, by losing me to her, you meant Carrie, not Maura. I told you she is nothing more than a friend regardless of her feelings for me. The only woman in my heart is you. No, Carrie had nothing to do with the redecoration of my space. That was all Cat, she surprised me with it when I returned from rehab. Now can we get back to being all over each other now, or do you really want to continue down this unimportant line of thinking?" he asked.

Molly sighed and kissed him and thankfully was able to let it go. Not that Shane gave her much time to dwell on anything but the feel of his fingers between her legs and his mouth over hers. He remembered just how she liked to be touched. Rough thrusts of his fingers inside of her, but light, playful forays over her clit with his thumb until her body clenched around him. The first of many orgasms she knew he was still capable of ringing from her.

Molly and Shane were content for the moment to let their bodies do the talking. There was still much to discuss between them, but for now, it could wait. They had forever together to fix what still needed to be fixed. Their love story was far from complete. In truth, it had only just begun.

EPILOGUE

If Rachel could cry, she would. She no longer had access to the world of the living. The gray had called her back. She had hoped for more time, but her duty was done. Maura was no more. Alexander, Claude, and Shane had found true love at last. The men she watched over for so many years no longer needed her protection. They weren't free of danger just yet. There were other things in store for them, but that was their concern. She could do no more for them. Not for the men and not for the women they loved.

Rachel thought about Molly. She'd tortured the poor girl a hundred times but hadn't honestly looked into her soul until the meeting with the Council. It had been more comfortable that way, seeing Molly as an adversary. A problem to be fixed instead of a lost girl with a higher purpose than just succumbing to the love of a man. Of them all, Molly's journey would prove to be even more treacherous. Her story was still to unfold. At least now she had some sense of her powers.

Rachel let everyone believe that it was Maura's powers within Molly. That hadn't been entirely true. Molly came from a long line of magic users. Her abilities buried after years of disuse and a lack of training. It was Molly who had brought herself back, her love for Shane had raised her from the dead. Maura had only put her head back on her body and opened the channel for Molly's magic to complete the rest.

Rachel could only hope that Molly continued to use her magic for good. That she returned to save her blessed sisters from their bondage and freed her people from the tyranny and persecution that had forced them into hiding. Alas, it was all beyond her influence at this point.

Rachel was free of her curse. She could finally move on. The light of the afterlife glowed in the near distance. With a heavy heart, Rachel moved towards it. Her time was up, she could finally rest. Despite her infatuation with Greg, she knew deep down he was meant for another. Rachel stepped into the light.

More From Stella Williams

Paranormal Romance & Urban Fantasy

<u>Maura's Men Trilogy</u>

Xander's Claim
Claude's Conquest
Shane's Redemption

<u>Secret of Ceres Series</u>

Ferocious
Dauntless
Earnest
Zenith

<u>Langsmith Shifter Shorts</u>

Coy Wolf
A Night Divine
Bird of Prey

<u>Bloodlines</u>

His Soul to Keep

Contemporary Romance

<u>Paramour Novellas</u>

Felling Bechet
Unforgettable Valentine

About the Author

Stella Williams is a Blogger and USA TODAY Bestselling Paranormal Romance & Urban Fantasy Author, who lives in Washington State. She has a degree in Anthropology from The University of California, Santa Cruz. Stella prides herself in using her studies to create diverse worlds and characters for her novels.

You can find more about Stella Williams on her website: www.serpentinecreative.com

Continue reading for an excerpt of

Ferocious

Secret of Ceres Book 1

“I have no idea what you are talking about.”

Farrah tried plausible deniability. She didn't have to work hard. Donovan Mars was attractive to her, but she wouldn't touch that stick in the mud with a ten-foot pole.

Jaq started to chuckle as he finished putting the groceries away.

“Funny, he said the same about you. Regardless if that were true, why is he at your door right now?”

Farrah opened her mouth to say something, but there was a knock at her door followed by a small flare of energy announcing that Donovan was in fact at her door. Jaq was closer than she was so he opened the door with a scowl on his face.

“You two need to find that pole you keep talking about because neither of you has one.”

Jaq walked out the door and down the hall before either Farrah or Donovan could speak. Farrah put her head out the door and waited until Jaq was in fact gone before glaring at Donovan.

“How dare you approach my brother without notifying me!”

Donovan shook his head.

“And risk you warning him I was coming. What kind of investigator would I be then?”

"I'm not saying you shouldn't have talked to him, but I am supposed to be your partner on this case. It would go a lot smoother if you let me know what leads you're working. That way we aren't doing twice the work for no reason other than your big ego!"

"My ego? This is not about my ego. This is about you being related to the suspect!"

"Suspect!"

One of Farrah's neighbors poked their head out of their door and turned to look in their direction. Farrah smiled and waved at the old woman before grabbing Donovan's collar and pulling him inside. The last thing they needed was to have anyone whispering about what they were up to. Farrah slammed the door behind them and leaned against it.

"My brother is not a suspect. He had nothing to do with Daphne's disappearance. You know that," Farrah said.

Her hands fisted at her sides.

"Your judgment can't be trusted."

Her nails bit into her palms as she fought the urge to smack the smug look from his face.

"My judgment about my brother or my judgment in general."

"Jaquis Andromeda stays a suspect until we find

evidence otherwise."

Farrah glared at Donovan. He glared back. Farrah's blood boiled with rage. She could feel the energy rising up from her core and dancing just below her skin. At this point, it wouldn't be enough for her to just calm down. She needed to redirect and focus that energy into something else, or better yet, someone else. Without a second thought, Farrah launched herself from the door and right at Donovan. He didn't have time to react before she pulled him down and pressed her lips to his. His facial hair tickled her chin and cheeks.

Donovan tensed for a moment. Farrah knew he would try to pull away and that was fine. It was only meant to be a chaste kiss. A way to channel her angry energy into something more pleasant and leave him the one on edge. Farrah wasn't expecting his strong arms to encircle her waist and pull her flush against his rock-hard body. Nor did she expect him to open his mouth and nip at her lip. Not out of anger, but an invitation. He moved his head back far enough to look her in the eye.

Donovan was angry, but the fires of passion danced in his eyes. Both of them stood stock still, trapped in the heat of the moment. Farrah's chest heaved as she warred with the dual sensations of fury and arousal. She knew Donovan did the same. Their natural energy swirled around them. They mixed and intertwined until Farrah could barely distinguish hers from his. Donovan bent lower, his lips were just shy of hers. So close she could feel his warmth against them.

He made no further move. Leaving the next step up

to Farrah. All she had

to do was lean in. Her body screamed for her to go for it, but Farrah's mind shouted for her to stop, to pull away. For once Farrah decided to listen to her brain. Her hands that had been gripping Donovan's shirt fell to her sides.

Farrah closed her eyes and took a deep breath. She could feel the charged air dissipating as the heat drained out of the moment. Her body wept for the loss of opportunity, but there was nothing Farrah could do about that now. She had to remember Donovan was not someone she could be that open with. Not now and not ever. She opened her eyes and playfully tugged Donovan's beard.

"Did you bring the case file?"

Donovan didn't miss a beat. He smirked and pulled the file from the shoulder bag she just realized he wore. She reached for it, but he held it out of her grasp.

"You show me yours, and I'll show you mine."

Farrah felt a gush of wetness between her legs. Her body still hadn't registered the cease and desist her brain stamped all over its urges when it came to Donovan Mars. She walked over to the coffee table and picked up Daphne's diary.

"We'll go over both together. I think we've established the lack of trust in this unfortunate partnership," Farrah said and gestured for him to sit on the couch.

"Trust is earned, Ms. Andromeda, and in the

short time I've known you, you've proven most untrustworthy."

"Likewise, Mr. Mars," she said, snatching the case file from his hands.

Donovan got comfortable on the couch leaving Farrah to take the case file over to the breakfast bar. There was plenty of space on the sofa, but Farrah didn't trust her brain to keep winning the battle with her body if she stayed close to him. It was going to be a long night.

Ferocious
Secret of Ceres Book 1
Available Now
www.serpentinecreative.com

www.ingramcontent.com/pod-product-compliance
Lightning Source LLC
Chambersburg PA
CBHW021332190726
48288CB00003B/1072